Jenny, Unravelled.

Pauline McLynn lives in Dublin with her husband, Richard, and two cats named Brenda and Alice. She used to have other cats too — Mutt, Geoff, Noel, Brendan, Snubby and Geezee. When she was growing up in Galway, in the west of Ireland, her family had dogs — Roberta, Lady Pink Weasel, Dennis and TD. Her brothers used to call her 'verruca head' and 'hook nose' (serio) but they don't do that any more, at least not to her face, which is good. She has a wonky, crackly right knee from doing Irish dancing (probably the wrong way!) when she was younger. Pauline still loves performing and is now an award-winning actor, perhaps best known for playing the roles of Mrs Doyle in *Father Ted* and Libby Croker in *Shameless*. She is also very good at knitting and has written eight other novels, but *Jenny Q* is her first series for teenagers.

Books by Pauline McLynn
JENNY Q, STITCHED UP!
JENNY Q, UNRAVELLED

Jenny Q, Unravelled

PAULINE McLYNN

PUFFIN

PUFFIN BOOKS

Published by the Penguin Group

Penguin Books Ltd, 80 Strand, London WC2R ORL, England

Penguin Group (USA) Inc., 375 Hudson Street, New York, New York 10014, USA

Penguin Group (Canada), 90 Eglinton Avenue East, Suite 700, Toronto, Ontario, Canada M4P 2Y3
(a division of Pearson Penguin Canada Inc.)

Penguin Ireland, 25 St Stephen's Green, Dublin 2, Ireland (a division of Penguin Books Ltd)

Penguin Group (Australia), 707 Collins Street, Melbourne, Victoria 3008, Australia
(a division of Pearson Australia Group Pty Ltd)

Penguin Books India Pvt Ltd, 11 Community Centre, Panchsheel Park, New Delhi – 110 017, India

Penguin Group (NZ), 67 Apollo Drive, Rosedale, Auckland 0632, New Zealand
(a division of Pearson New Zealand Ltd)

Penguin Books (South Africa) (Pty) Ltd, Block D, Rosebank Office Park, 181 Jan Smuts Avenue, Parktown
North, Gauteng 2193, South Africa

Penguin Books Ltd, Registered Offices: 80 Strand, London WC2R ORL, England

puffinbooks.com

First published 2013
001

Text copyright © Pauline McLynn, 2013
Illustrations copyright © Kate Jenkins and Puffin Books, 2013
All rights reserved

The moral right of the author and illustrator has been asserted

Set in 12/18pt Gill Sans
Printed in Great Britain by Clays Ltd, St Ives plc

British Library Cataloguing in Publication Data
A CIP catalogue record for this book is available from the British Library

ISBN: 978-0-141-34151-4

www.greenpenguin.co.uk

ALWAYS LEARNING   **PEARSON**

For Emily White,
a v neglected, teenage god-child

DUDE!

There's only one way to say this – babies are full of shizz. Top to toe FULL OF IT. We got a new one before Xmas and his name is Harry. He is the best little bundle of gurgles and chuckles and POO. I can't believe the amount that comes out of his tiny little body. In the beginning it was very green and sticky. Now it's very yellow and sticky. And not massively *solid*. Though it looks quite massive in general after he's dumped it in his nappy. He smells yummy for a while and then his little face goes all red, nearly maroon* and you just know looking at him that he's

---

* The colour of my school uniform and therefore not a GREAT colour.

depositing something fairly vile for a family member to take care of.

See, that's also the thing with babies: they get *help* with *everything*. They do virtually nothing in return, except capture your heart and make you love them. It's like we're staff. Not that I mind: Harry is the BEST.

Ennyhoo, there he is with his little maroon face looking like he's concentrating on something that's really hard to figure out and along comes the smell, and Harry somehow looks like he's smiling, and you know it's time for a change of undies for Harry Quinn, otherwise he'll holler the house down like he's being tortured.

Oh, nearly forgot to mention that he's fond of spewing up all over himself too, and anyone else around or under him, at random times. Like, right now he's hanging over Dermot's shoulder (that's my older bruv) and he's just opened his mouth and puked down Derm's back, then a stretch of his little fisty fists and he's asleep again. He has managed to miss the towel on our brother's shoulder, carefully placed there to catch such emissions. What an aim! SHOT! No one tells you just how much goo comes out of a baby, all ends, and what joy they seem to take in their efforts. Goo, poo, wee – Harry's full of the stuff.

His belches are a mighty big sound too.

There's no predicting Harry. Gran says we can't ever 'second guess' him because 'he's been here before'. Clearly Harry has not been here before, he's very new to the place, but my gran is as crazy as the rest of the Quinn family, so you gotta roll with that (trust me, let it wash over you, do not resist, for resistance is futile). I should know: I'm one of them. I'm Jennifer Quinn, of the crazy Quinns of Oakdale, Dublin, and a middle child now, since the lil bro arrived.

> I'm Jenny Q[†]
> How do you do?
> Welcome to my world of puke and poo!

OK, should explain that too – me and my Besties (Dixie and Uggs) are kinda doin' a poetry jam after school from time to time. Hence me *RHYMES*. And 'riddums', as one of my gran's MAD friends calls them. It's a good laugh and we all resist criticism of anyone's efforts so it's v positive too, which can't be bad!

---

† That's Jenny with a *y* not Jenny with an *i* = v v important detail.

So, the Quinns have officially gone gaga. Yes, I know some of you would argue that this was always the case BUT I speak of a super-mega-gaganess. It's understandable, though, because as I have explained Harry Quinn is a little gem and the most beautiful baby in the world – I'm not usually a boastrel but that is one solid factoid.

And it's not just us Quinns who've gone a bit loopy for the babe, my brother's group Ten Guitars[‡] are all well into the lil dude: Harry is their official mascot. Actually he got born v early just so as he could be their lucky charm – he was meant to stay 'inside' a while longer but one television appearance by the group on *Teen Factor X* and Harry was out and in the middle of the action. He's clearly a kid with attitude, big 'tude, if his birth is anything to go by.

All in all, Harry is making his small presence felt in a big way.

The Quinns now speak a different language at home from the rest of the world at large. It's all 'Wot does da liggle fellah want?' and 'Whodabestest boy in the whole wide world? Iddit Hawwy? Iddit? *Iddit?*' Idiot, more like,

‡ They play guitars and there are ten of them = says it all as to how and why, really . . .

because that's what he's made of all of us. Then we tickle his toes and it's hard not to take a bite of his chubby little legs cos he's so cute. My gran goes 'coocheecoochee coo' a lot to him and he seems to know what she means because he kind of gurgles[6] at her in response.

After his bath each evening it's a treat to get to blow raspberries on his tummy, and he loves that. Harry has the softest skin *ever* in the history of *very* soft skin.

He does a good line in stretches too. Mum says it's his baby version of t'ai chi. And sometimes it's a bit jerky, so that's when we know he's practising his kung fu moves.

I LOVE IT ALL!

And to think I wasn't all that thrilled when I heard the news that I was going to have a baby brother. Was I nuts?

Oh, and the house smells all baby powder lovely now too. Well, that is, it smells lovely and babyish when Harry isn't doing a jobby in his nappy, because that's the darkly odorous side of human beings, whatever size they may be.

6 He's clearly v advanced for such a small chap.

TRASH

Today I'm in the kitchen with Harry, in charge of babysitting for a while because Mum is having a well-earned snooze. She has to breastfeed Harry every two hours and he can take his own sweet time if he has a mind to, dawdling while enjoying his surroundings. I still get a *leeetle* bit wobbly seeing my mum's chesticles every so often and I'm totes *MORTO* if anyone outside of the family espies them. Dad says Harry's a clever little chap because he won't get a proper 'go' at boobies again till he's ancient – EUW, DAD! Way, *way* too much information right there.

Don't worry, Gran is lurking and keeping an eye on me, supervising my babysitting, so there's no need to call Social Services just yet. And I would NEVER let ANY harm come to Harry on my watch, no WAY, not EVER. As I think of it, Gran is around a lot right now. OK, it is the Yuletide season, which is big time family time, and she does live in what used to be our garage (!), but even so she's *everywhere* since Harry arrived. I should probs wonder *Why?* more but I am distracto in the head.

Reason? I can hear Dermot and some of his friends strumming their guitars in the lounge and it makes my heart do funny jumps. Stevie Lee Bolton is in there. He's one of the Guitars. He is the fittest guy in Oakdale, where we live, and he's sixteen and probably thinks I'm a squirt — well, of course he does, how could he not? I'm thirteen and he's an older generation — they always see the youngsters as eejits and nuisances if they even truly notice us at all. It is the way of things and always has been since the dawn of time, I'd say.

Steve Bolton has deep brown eyes and floppy, curly hair and I can't really get past that now as I imagine him in my mind — in other words the kind of looks that can mesmerize a gal (me!). He is seriously, meltingly gorgeous. My chest hurts a bit thinking about him. Dixie once remarked that I might be bewitched.*

Ennyhoo, we recently celebrated the New Year so I'm thinking of my annual Things To Do List. I love lists. I have a pen with a red feather on top that writes in turquoise sparkly ink and it's lined up on the kitchen table beside a totes cute notebook that Dixie gave me for Christmas, ready to take my instructions to myself for the next twelve months. I don't want to call them 'resolutions' because those always seem doomed to failure in the world of Jenny Q: 'Just asking for trouble,' as Gran would say. So it's a list of Things To Do or *suggestions*, as Dixie has proposed we call them this year.

'We' is the Gang = me (Jennifer Margaret Anne Quinn), Dorothy 'Dixie' Purvis and Eugene 'Uggs' Nightingale.

Uggs's dog, Gypsy Nightingale, is NOT one of the Gang, though she tries to muscle (her wiry, pongy self) in at every turn.

Harry has just been changed and he's got a sleepy look on his face, so I'll put him in his cradle for a snooze.

* oh, hang on, maybe she said I might be-a-witch – can't remember.

Trash

He needs a lot of sleep because he's busy growing and eating and so on. I can't resist giving him a little volley of kisses on his lovely little face. I hear someone clearing his throat and, when I look, it's Stevie Lee Bolton. EEP! I hope my hair[†] isn't sticking out too much and that my face isn't too red from my baby duties.

'I'm in charge of making coffee for the Guitars,'[‡] he says and goes to fill the kettle.

My legs are feeling tingly and I think I'd probably best sit down before I fall over.

'You know where everything is, don't you?' My voice sounds thin and squeaky. My behind is clenched up with embarrassment.

'How's the little guy?'

'Great. Time for his snooze,' I say and put the baby down.

My hand immediately goes to my hair to check on what kind of thatch is rockin' a look up there. I can't decide if I can feel product or grease. There's a bit of an

---

† It's a strawberry blonde, NOT ginger, and can have a mind of its own if I take my attention off it for even a nanosecond.

‡ It's totes hip and cool to call the group the Guitars rather than Ten Guitars which is, like, way formal and for outsiders.

9

awkward silence in the kitchen now because I don't know what to say next. It doesn't seem to bother Stevie Lee, but then again he is older and *way* cool, so nothing really gets to him. My heart is thundering in my chest and I have a weird ringing in my ears. Surely he can hear all that? I want the floor to open and swallow me.

The kettle rumbles to a boil and clicks off.

SLB is looking at me in a strange way.

'Err, Jen,'[6] he says.

'Yes?'

'Is there a reason why Harry is in the recycling box?'

WHAT??!!!

I look and, sure enough, my tiny baby brother is sleeping soundly on top of a pile of newspapers in the box next to his cradle. He looks v v comfortable but that doesn't take away from the fact that I, his one and only sister, put him in the trash. Harry might have been thrown out into the green bin!

If this is discovered I'll never be allowed to look after the baby ever again.[§]

---

6 My name sounds so lovely when he says it!

§ I am not fit to be left in charge, either. I am rubbish, not Harry.

EEK!

I am in a total fluster now – who wouldn't be?!

SLB is looking calm, as if this is normal – It's *so not*! I nearly threw my baby brother in the bin. In fact, I kind of did, seeing as how he was in the recycling box when spotted, clean as that bin is. I check his Babygro for print marks* because we, the Quinn family, are big into all things criminal and detective and that would be a totes giveaway if this case ever gets to court. EEK!!!!

I was so busy trying to look cool for Steve Bolton,

---

* If there's a newspaper story even part-printed on his lil bod, then it can be identified and dated and I can be banged up for a crime I *SO DID* commit = v ungood . . .

going, 'See how it's, like, *so* second nature to me to look after Harry that I don't even need to check where I'm putting him as I lay him down,' that I *messed up* on the baby's actual location. Not good. Unacceptable. V v (v) bad.

Dire, actually. Totes DIRE.

'We will never speak of this,' Bolton says, trying not to smile.

'Thank you.' I remain formal because this is an important moment in life, as well as in our non-existent relationship. 'So we are agreed? And no harm has come to anyone.'

'Agreed.'

I am *scarlet*, I just know it and MORTO too, and a vile creeping creature upon the face of the earth to do such a thing to a newborn babe.

Gran shuffles in. I drag in a breath and hold it = painful. Will Stevie Lee shop me to the adult(ish) person actually in charge? Now that I think of it, where was she when I needed her? EH?

Bolton keeps to the party line and says nothing.[†] He

† I am even more enthralled with him now - a man of moral fibre, dependableness* and loyalty. * Yes, I made that word up.

just continues coffee-making. Gran, though, can *smell* situations, so I worry what she'll get up to. However, surely she knows that I totally fancy Bolton?[‡] I may never know the (surely awful) truth, but she cuts me some slack and only asks, 'How goes it all?' We mutter nonsense that sounds like an answer.

Gran then glances at me and says, 'Jen, you really should put Harry down in his cradle if he's sleeping, otherwise he'll get into terribly bad habits and want to be held all the time.'

I have to bite my tongue because if I tell her exactly why I'm holding the baby, she might banish me from my duties for evermore.

'K,' I say and pop the lil dude into his official bed. He's not a bit bothered, doesn't even give a sigh.

Gran is scouring the kitchen with some dark purpose, i.e. it looks like she's considering rustling up some food. This is bad news for anyone who'll have to eat the bizarro concoction she comes up with – once she boiled an egg and the Fire Brigade had to be called, no kidding: one of the more epic failures on a list of truly

[‡] It's mortifying to think it might be apparent . . . even to a granny . . .

competitive failures for the Quinn family. Her last effort here in the main house was a liver curry (*imagine!*) because she thought Mum 'needed iron'. We had no idea what had happened until we were sitting in front of the 'meal' and it was too late to retreat or escape the potentially deadly Connie Curry.

'Interesting,' Dad said, though without tasting the mix. The smell of it was darkly pungent and threatening enough to put him off that.

The rest of us were stifling screams.

Gran had a mouthful and said, 'This doesn't taste right.'

There was almost an audible family sigh as we all edged our plates further away from us, hoping that was the end of the incident and we could have chips and eggs and forget the horror.

Gran went to the fridge and came back with a large tub of orange yoghurt and added it to the curry, tasted it again and declared it a delight.

Here's the weirdest thing – it did make the thing taste edible . . . v v strange indeed.

Still, it's no reason to encourage her culinary adventures, truly.

'TIS THE SEASON

My phone beeps a text: **bah humbug! Am running away from home**. It's Dixie.

I reply: **c u in 10?**

And get: **make it 5!**

Dermot arrives to help Stevie Lee to carry the Guitars' coffees and they disappear. Gran is still skulking.

'Why do I feel you're acting shifty?' she muses, catching my eye in a searching way that I so don't love. I'm not sure how adults do it, but they can *sniff* controversy or a 'situation'. I play dumb – eh, *obvs* – and I'm not sure if I want her to think it's my crushmostpash for SLB that's at the heart of this shiftiness she senses or the fact that I chucked my beautiful new bro in the bin. Such choices can leave a gal entirely between a rock and a hard place. I am saved by a v v melodramatic entrance by my bestest galpal, Dixie.

'All this cheery happiness and good will to all men is killing me,' she declares. 'Plus my dork brother,* who I *swear* must be adopted and not related to me, drank a bottle of something pink and vile and is holed up in our loo as a result, so that's out of bounds now. Maybe for evermore.'

'Full-sized Kit Kat, so?' I enquire.

'Totes. And immédiatement – if not sooner!'

This means she's in a genuine crisis. Ordinary snackage can be dealt with by a two-finger bar, but four . . . well, that's major, that's *need* not just *want*.

'Plus, we're down to the crapola chocs in the Christmas boxes in our house now,' she says.

I shiver. 'Coffee flavoured?'†

'Yup. And *nougat*.' Her voice is dripping scorn as she elongates the word *noogah*. 'YUCK! NOOGACK! Who

---

* Everyone agrees that he's a delinquent.

† I like coffee itself, but chocs with coffee-flavoured centres are gack.

in their right minds ever thought that was a good thing to invent?'

'And hello to you too, Dixie,' says Gran.

Dixie sighs, v dramatically, and says, 'Happy festive season to you and to us all.' Her heart is *so* not in it, in fact she's leaking insincerity, though I'm sure she'd pass it off as fabliss irony if quizzed.

Of course, one of the reasons Dix is in such doodah form is that she's got lurve problems. She was snogging Jason 'the Tongue' Fielding for a while and, even though she says it counts for nothing, I think she really does like him. Then, out of the blue, he only went and posted a pic of them snogging on Facebook AND tagged her in it, *without express and prior permission*. She was v UNpleased,[‡] to say the least. Guys don't GET stuff sometimes, which is another of life's trials.

We both try to stare Gran out of it so that she'll leave us to a good goss in the kitchen, but there's no shifting her. In fact, if I had money to bet on it, I'd say she's doing this deliberately. She is v experienced at being:

---

‡ Natch.

a) an adult, as she is ancient, and

b) annoying, because she is an adult.[6]

She grants us a big beam and says, 'I'm getting ready for my poker night,' so we know she's going nowhere else fast.

'Dixie,' I start, but she suddenly raises her hand and says:

'Sorry, can't concentrate, Baby Harry in the room!'

I understand it completely – that lil guy has an *effect* on us women. He's swoontastic! And I don't think he even knows it.

'Wake him and you die,' I tell her, although I don't mean it, because I love it when he's awake and doing his stretchies and gurglies.

So, we stand like two eejits whispering stuff into his cradle. It beats leaning over the recycling box by many miles, but that is an observation I keep to myself.

6 It comes with the whole adult/grown-up territory, I think.

18

SEEING RED

We have the makings of a party now and, you know, it *is* the season to be jolly and all that. There's guitar music coming from the next room and I've rustled up some tasties for Dix and I. That means it's almost inevitable that next door's dog will sense what's going on. She does. Her radar is impressive, though I will never say this aloud in case it seems like I'm praising her, a thing I refuse to do . . . in *any* way. I hear yippy barking and, as the kitchen door opens, a ratty-sized thing runs in, all jigging about and doing a doggy smile. It's Gypsy followed by Eugene Nightingale, our other Bestie and third member of the Gang.

The dog is in a red hooded coat that Uggs knitted

her for Christmas. She thinks she's *IT* in it. So does everyone, except me. I don't think they realize what I *know*, which is: that dog is 'up to something'. Tragically, I am often the butt end of that 'something'. We will never see eye to eye, her and I, except for those times when she literally brings me down to her own low level by making me fall over.*

'Ah, me jewel and darlin' Gypsy,' says Gran, who gets on v well with the mutt. 'Eugene, I presume she'll be attending my poker night?'

'Oh yes, she's looking forward to it very much,' says Uggs.

I can only shake my head at the madness of them discussing that varmint critter like she's one of us. She is not and never will be. End of.

'I'll take her little coat off, Eugene, or she won't feel the good of it when she goes outside again.'

'Good thinking,' Uggs says. 'I don't want her catching cold.'

WHAT???? Are they insane?

'If she wakes Harry, she's toast,' I tell Uggs. I hope he hears the sincerity in this statement – in fact, I will

* one of her fave pastimes and v vexing for me.

actually call it a threat if anyone asks. Sadly, they don't.

I shoo the beast away and growl at her a bit for good measure. She skips off, ignoring me. Then I catch her eye and I swear she's actually laughing at me in a kinda grinny, terrier way. It's insufferable and I can't believe no one else notices it.

We need a bit of Gang time so Gran takes over Harry-minding duty. We load up on snacks (including the medicinal Kit Kat for Dixie) and head to my room in the hope of some privacy. Not that the Quinns ever TRULY respect a closed door – to this crazed family, it's a challenge, as if there's *certainly* something worth snooping on in the room with the closed door. Sheesh!†

Uggs wants to leave the door open – is he *mad*? Apparently he feels Gypsy would like to divide her time between Gran and Harry downstairs and us in my room. He almost says, 'She's part of the Gang too,' but catches my face doing my 'don't go there, Eugene' in a

---

† OK, OK, sometimes even I am part of the 'let's see what's behind that tightly closed door' brigade, but it's genetic: I am BRED to do it and therefore I say it's not my fault . . . well, not much my fault anyhow . . .

21

v v expressive way and he lets the matter drop. I close the door.

'I need a Faceboast,' Dixie says before we've even called the meeting to order. 'I need to be pursued publicly by a hunky hottie and to wipe Jason Fielding's face in it and be all fabulously fab in general.'

'Is that all?' I say, kinda smirking.

She shoots me a *LOOK* and goes, 'YES – do we have a problem with this impossibly brilliant plan?'

'Uh-*uh*,' I say, 'with you all the way, Dix.'

Uggs is nodding like a, well, v v noddy thing – one of those toy dogs on the back shelf of a car maybe – and going, 'Yes, yes, all the way, Dix.'

'The v good news is that I saw him *by accident* today and he's got spots – could be too much choccy over the last week or, more hopefully, the onset of long-lasting teenage acne.'

Something about the way she says she *accidentally* saw the Tongue makes me nervous.

'Are you stalking Jason Fielding?' I ask, quietly and carefully.

Dix gives a v forced laugh and says, 'Don't be ridic, Jen.'

So she probably is, then – EEEK!

'More good news is that no one has hooked up with him datewise since I dumped him, so he's a saddo on the shelf.'

Uggs and I 'eep' gently at this, because we're singularly on that sadsville shelf too. And strictly speaking so is Dix, but this is SO not the time to point that out to her.

And, while I'm at it, both Uggs and I are prone to outbreaks of spots, so it's v insensitive of Dix to mention acne or any of its zitty cousins.

'Jen, fire up the computer. I'm going online to announce my availability and therefore lure a suitor.'

'Now THAT is a v v BAD idea,' Uggs says. 'Maybe the worst idea in the history of bad ideas.'

'J'agree,' I say. 'Très not good, Dix.'

'I am a pioneer,' she tells us loftily. 'I lead the way, take initiative. Most of all, je refuse to give up on l'amour.‡ And there's no way I want to have to settle for dating one of the dorks we go to school with, or any other dork within the general Oakdale area for that matter.'

‡ Does anyone else think that some things sound better in le français? To introduce a certain je ne sais quoi?

She has a point about the lack of serious romantic talent in our world, apart from Stevie Bolton, who is in a different league anyhow.

'It's what social media is for,' she concludes. 'And I might put a lonely-hearts dating notice in the local schools' newspaper too,'[6] she adds after a pause.

I try not to look too horrified. I have to bite my tongue rather than point out that a mere breath ago she said she didn't want to date any of our school-dorks or even local dorks – that's Dixie, though, a mass of contradictions and it is v V unwise to draw attention to it. I want to wash my hands of the bonkers scheme, but she's my bestest galpal so I have to go along with it. Uggs follows suit, looking glum. Another galling point is that if this goes bumcheeks up and Dixie gets landed with a geek, Gypsy will be blameless, as the mutt is not at the meeting, the cunning wretch. I should have stayed downstairs minding Harry.

6 The lonely-hearts section in our local schools' rag started a year or so ago. If I remember rightly, the Gang were all in agreement that it was the saddest of sad sections and we would never be caught dead even glancing at the page . . .

24

'Well, the enthusiasm I'm feeling in this room is altogether underwhelming,' Dixie says. 'I am fighting injustice here and need the support of my nearests. Which is you two. So look lively and get with the programme.'

IT'S COMPLICATED

'So, we need to talk up my glamazingness,' Dixie tells us. 'I'm thinking we should word the lonely hearts something like, "Stunning teen, GSOH,* seeks slightly older, handsome man for friendship and laughter." What do you think?'

I'm not *loving* the use of 'we' here. *At all.* I shrug and make an unimpressed face. I am trying to have as little to do with this as possible. If I engage with Dixie on this scheme, *I* might end up going on a date as her guinea pig, if she just doesn't like the look of whatever Lonely Heart

---

* Most of the time it is fair to say Dixie does have a good sense of humour, but sometimes she can be plain bonkers . . .

turns up. Nothing is beyond the Dix and there are no lows to which she will not let me stoop on her behalf.[†]

'As for Facebook, I'll change my status from "It's complicated" to "Single" and accept lots of new friend requests. That should get the ball rolling.'

'It's still complicated,' Uggs mutters and he's not wrong.

'I may also need a make-over – discuss.'

'It's v v important to look stunning in case you chance upon the Tongue in your travels,' I say, bearing in mind she may also be deliberately putting herself in the way of said person!

'Am I hearing highlights?' she asks.

'The school aren't keen on anything wild or too colourful,' Uggs points out.[‡]

'Subtlety is my middle name,' Dixie says, without even a trace of irony.[⑥]

[†] I know this instinctually, or as Gran would say, 'I feel it in me waters,' and *ugh* I so wish she wouldn't!

[‡] Oakdale High doesn't even allow us to eat smelly crisps on the school grounds any more, let alone have mad hairdos or piercings.

[⑥] Subtle is not in her DNA, not even a little, not a *jot*.

Uggs clears his throat and I think it's to disguise a laugh.

'New perfume is a must,' I say. 'The sort that wafts in before you and lingers after you've gone, leaving a tantalizing breath of Dixie behind.'

'You know, Jen, that is almost genius,' she says. 'I'll be unmissably snifftastic.'

'Have you unfriended Jason Fielding?' I ask.

'Don't be ridic, Jen, I have to be aware of his every move. Keep your friends close and your enemies closer and all that. Besides, he's unaware of my vast wrath, so when the time comes I'll slay him with fabulosity and disdain and he won't see it coming – it's a foolproof plan.'

I *almost* feel sorry for the Tongue, because he has no idea what he has unleashed upon himself, the poor gormless eejit.

Uggs makes an attempt to talk sense into Dixie. He can get all grown-up sometimes and even though that can seem a bit stuffy and *old*, I'm glad of it right now. He's a bit of a swot too, and that's useful during school time.

'I saw a really interesting article that might help you get through this,' he says.

Dixie narrows her eyes and goes, 'Oh yeah?' Not in a *great* way.

'Deffo, yeah.'

Poor Uggs, I'd say he's sweating now with nerves at how this might go! Still, he's in the eye of the storm and has to continue.

'It was a list of the fifteen things you should give up on to live a happy life.'

Dixie snorts. 'Fifteen? I'm not sure I have those hours of my life left, Uggs, to give up so many things. Bet they're all good things too. Is chocolate on the list?'

Uggs is scarlet now. 'It's not that kind of list, not material things, it's more attitudes and, erm, habits.'

'Par example, s'il vous plaît?'

'Well, it says you should give up on the past, for instance, because the present and the future are more important and obsessing about the past just holds you back. And give up on blame too, because that's such a negative.'

Dixie holds up a hand to stop him. 'Uggs, that would just lead to people getting away with bad shizz.'

'It might not,' he counters, trying to stick to his point.

I can see he's wavering, though. Dixie is hard to argue with.

'You're just giving people permission to do bad things and then wipe the slate with the excuse that it's all in the past,' she says.

'Food for thought,' I say, trying to help, though I'm not sure who. It's a fairly pathetic try one way or another and they both ignore me.

'Tell you what, I'll consider the fifteen things when I'm fifteen, how about that? Until then, it's "stick up for Dixie" time.'

ENTERPRISE

'Seems weird to be sitting around talking without a project to work on,' Uggs says.

We have a Knit 'n' Knatter Club within the Gang and usually have items or gifts to make on our needles as we work out life and the universe and so on. Uggs mentioning this is, of course, another ruse to get Dixie off her obsession with her ex and her latest bonkers plan to deal with it. Fair play to him for a valiant effort, though I suspect there's no thwarting Dixie from her new fave topic.

I should say at this point that I didn't think Dixie and Jason Fielding were ever a solid, romantic item. They weren't exactly dating, as far as *I* was aware. They had a loose arrangement to get off with each other and do some unwatchable snogging on Youth Club nights. I suspect she's talking it up now for drama's sake, plus there's no doubt that she has been scorned and that he crossed a line by Faceboasting a pic of the aforementioned unwatchable snogging. Mind you, he did always get away with calling her 'babe', in spite of her saying she'd thump him if he ever did, so perhaps there was a smidgen of something more going on. Sheesh, lurve stuff is exhausting!

'We need to make some moolah,' Dixie says. 'Highlights and makeovers don't come free.'

We all give sigh because:

a) yes, we're smashed broke due to the expense of the festive season's gifting, and

b) it means Dixie is about to burst into action and we'll need serious energy to keep up.

'I'm thinking Valentine's Day,' she says.

She's a One Hit Wonder right now when it comes to love and all its relatives.

'How about we knit and stuff hearts and sell

them at school, like we did Uggs's bath bombs for Christmas.'

It's a v good idea.

'They don't all have to be red, because maybe people will want to get them for friends or themselves as a love treat. We can use any oddments we have left from last year and even do stripes if we have to.' Dixie is a Teenpreneur, fureshure!

'We can do heart-shaped bath bombs if we get a heart-shaped bun tin or a biscuit cutter,' Uggs suggests.

Another brillig idea!

The Gang is back in business and I can look forward to boosting my stash o' cash = hooray!

Dixie snorts. '*NO ONE* says "bun" or "biscuit" any more, Uggs. It's all cupcakes and cookies now. Sometimes you are such a doofus.'

Uggs reddens up but he doesn't mind.

Then Dixie drops her most serious bombshell. 'As part of my makeover, I'll have to lose a few pounds. I'm carrying some festive jetlag weight – it's the stress of spending too much time with my family in a confined space.'

EEEEK! Dixie never goes on a regime alone: we'll be expected to row in too.

'That would be "die" with a *t* on the end of it,' Uggs checks.

'Yes.'

Dixie leaves the room with a flounce and we mull over our new circumstances.

'We needn't panic,' Uggs assures me. 'She'll keep it up for a week, max.'

'Are you sure about that?' I ask.

'No,' he admits. 'But if past attempts are anything to go by, she'll hardly even last a full week.'

'I hope you're right.'

'The only trouble is that Dixie gets quite cranky when she's hungry.' So do I. So does Uggs.

And our parents and teachers would go nuts if they knew we were dieting, because it's a no-no round these parts, in case anyone thinks it's in any way a good idea and maybe takes it too far. And that's quite right, because anorexia is NOT a good thing, *ever*, even if Dixie did once declare she wouldn't mind having it just for a few days. We get regular lectures about not believing that thin is good and the word Thinspiration is outlawed because it is bad to glorify a deliberately skinny role model – we should just be the normal size we are meant to be. People come in all shapes and sizes: fact.

Dixie returns with some news. 'Obviously, a two-fingered Kit Kat is allowed on our new regime. Daily.'

So, it's not all doom and gloom . . . I suppose . . . even if she did say 'our', so we are deffo tied in, and we can have the chocolate/biscuit bar of the gods. Life is a squiggly road full of hazards and twistiness.

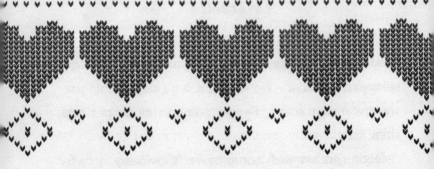

FORE!

The downstairs of Quinn HQ is buzzing as the Guitars are leaving, so I quickly slap on some lip gloss and run a brush through my hair. I hear a mild crackling, which means my hair is now electric, in the wrong way, and there's not a lot that can be done with that in a hurry. I bet it looks like a frightened gorse bush planted on my head. Still, I can't miss an opp to be seen by the latest and hippest Dublin boy band. The hallway is heaving with young men and would be quite a sight if they were all as F.I.T. as Stevie Lee Bolton but, tragically, they are not.

For example, there's Gary O'Brien, who is a dork. He seems to be convinced he's a badass from a 'hood and wears his jeans v low, with a beanie constantly plopped on his head. The day he opts for a hairnet or a headscarf is the day we will have to shoot him or get him permanently grounded in his home. He insists on greeting his 'homies' by riffling fingers followed by a fist bump, and high-fiving everyone else and calling them 'bro' or 'sistah'! Strangely, though, the lustre that Ten Guitars has brought to all in the group has almost made even him* seem cool. *Almost.*

Mum comes sleepily down the stairs, followed by Dad, and I cringe that anyone might think they've been up to anything in their room. It's not such a stretch of the imagination to think such a thing, what with them recently producing a new baby and all. So, it probably looks a bit racy and that makes me boil with embarrassment. The fact is they are both so tired from waking with Harry during the night since he arrived that they sleep whenever they have an opportunity.

Well, sometimes Dad plays golf in the house too. He got a Wii game for Christmas and he's obsessed with it. All we hear from the TV room when he's in there is him shouting 'fore', which is mad, because that's what

* A *mahoosive* ee jit.

you do on an actual golf course if you've hit a ball the wrong way and need to warn people ahead to duck. We told him there's no need to do it when it's a virtual game, but he says if he's ever rich enough to take up the real thing, he'll need to get used to shouting 'fore', because he's not very good at golf.

I'm glad the Guitars are leaving, because Mum getting up now means a feed for the baby and that means her buzooms will be out and there's only so much of my mum that I want those older guys seeing! Or me for that matter – I'd prefer not to have to behold her breastage if poss.

Gypsy trots up to the crowd as if to say goodbye. She's now wearing a sequinned dicky bow and everyone tells her she's gorgeous. I really can't figure out how she has everyone wrapped around her hairy paws, because she's not in any way cute. Uggs says she's a happy, smiling dog and that's why everyone loves her. I think she's a two-faced, yappedy scrap of fur, but I'll admit she looks *quite* nice in the dicky bow – I know, I know, I must be going soft in my old (teen)age.

Some of the Guitars are out on the road as the next lot of revellers arrive to party chez nous. It's

Gran's poker pals. Now the reason for Gypsy's bow tie is obvs. The oldies are all dressed up for a James Bond themed night. Happily, it's not as sore a sight as their *Sound of Music* night – put it this way, nuns in veils will never look the same to me again, and I wasn't even so taken with them in the first place. However, as Dixie points out, they could do *The Rocky Horror Picture Show* and that would be the end of everyone who caught sight of it and give new meaning to the term HORROR, because they'd all be running around in women's lingerie, be they men or women = v v gruesome. The very thought of this stirs the Kit Kat within me, in a dodgy way.

The wrinklies are, frankly, a mad bunch. Most of them hobble in or have walking sticks to help them along, but Francie Dolan is in a mobility scooter that he calls the Beast. There should be a driving test to use one of those things, because Francie is downright dangerous in his. Tonight he's got a white toy cat on his lap, like one of the Bond villains.

'Blofeld,' Uggs tells me, because he is part nerd and a big fan of James Bond.

'Your head is full of miscellaneous[†] nonsense,' I say, which is both a good and a bad thing.

He nods. 'Yup, it's a busy place.' He's clearly taken it as a compliment.

Connie's[‡] Cackling Cronies proceed to MORTIFY me by fluffing up my hair and sending it rampantly rampant.

'I haven't seen such a lovely head of curly red hair in ages,' says Mimsy Farrell.

I silently beg the floor to split in two and swallow me (and her!). Gran's pals are a social liability.

Now, the law of embarrassment states that one mortification will lead to another and they will multiply in awfulness as they meet each other, and so it is that Stevie Lee Bolton has just appeared, guitar in hand. He's grinning all over his gorge face.

'It *is* lovely hair, Jen,' he says and I think I might faint. He has done me another kindness and it's nearly too much for my overwrought self.

I want to scream, 'I am not a redhead or ginger,' for

† 'Miscellaneous' is a great word: like 'random' and 'et cetera', it covers a lot of ground, which I v love.

‡ AKA Gran.

all the world to know, but I'm also giddy that I got a compliment from a totes hot guy and therefore I have temporarily lost the ability to speak in anything but a gurgle. I go, '*GUH*,' at Steve and, when he's gone, Dixie chuckles and says, 'J'amaze – smooth, Jengirl.'[6]

I give her a dig in the ribs.

Of course they're not quite done with making a SHOW of me, because one of Gran's cronies says, 'And you're such a tiny little cutie too.'

I am not a tall thirteen-year-old but I'm not freakishly small either, so I boil some more.

'I think "petite" is the word you're looking for,' Uggs says.

He is being my saviour, of course, but the oldies just chuckle and go, '*AW*,' and that simply adds to all the embarrassment. Uggs is *scarlet* (natch). At least SLB wasn't around for that bit, which is scant mercy, but a mercy none the less.

The poker group moves on to Harry's crib and they *loom* over him, the poor mite. It strikes me that the world has to be a v scary place for a small, new baby, because everyone leans over into your personal space

---

6 As in *so* totally *not* smooth or cool!

41

and makes noises and stupid faces, and we must all look HUGE and lunatic as a result.§ Harry is still asleep, so he doesn't have to acknowledge the madsers by even looking at them, which would (surely) lead to him crying with fright and breaking all of our hearts.

Then Gran herds them into her flat, telling them all to watch out for Gypsy: 'She's a card shark.'

Eh, no, Gran, she's a *dog* . . .

Deez NUTS!

---

§ And a lot of people actually are!

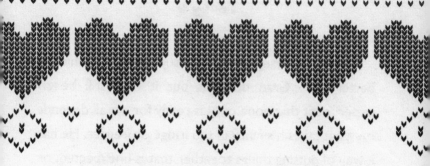

MUM'S THE WORD

Mum is still in her pyjamas. She doesn't get out of them much these days. And she looks worn out, shrunken. She's still got a bumpy-out tummy where Harry used to live, but her face is carved-looking with sharp angles that weren't there before. It's sort of like an invasion of bodysnatchers has happened and what we've been left with is a shell that's still Mum, but Mum Lite. She'll bounce back, I'm sure – it's just strange that she's so quiet and tired all the time.* And her eyes look sparkly yet hollow, like she's ecstatic and the opposite all at once.

* Note to self: must keep an eye on this and make sure to talk to Dad if things don't improve.

Dad takes charge of getting supper ready, which is better than Gran doing it but it may still be an experiment that none of us is ready for – it all depends on what takes his fancy in the fridge or freezer. He has a way of putting things together that is unexpected, or 'eclectic' as he calls it.

I love words and try to learn new ones all the time, so 'eclectic' got written in my notebook of good ones – it simply means mixing things up, really, but it sounds great, as well as being unusual for everyday conversation.[†]

Dad works with words because he's in advertising, but he often uses them to persuade people to buy a product they don't want or need, so there's an element of jiggery-pokery there if you ask me. And if I'm plain cross with him, I tell him he works on 'the Dark Side', but he merely brushes it off, saying he's putting bread on the table, food in our mouths, clothes on our backs, a roof over our heads, et cetera, et cetera. He really can go on and on (and on) with examples of all he does for us when it suits him.

Dermot got on his high horse about that once

† Well, any convo I seem to have.

during a heated clan row and said, 'You feel the end justifies the means?' and Dad coolly said, 'In this instance, yes.' And Dermot muttered, 'I was only doing my job,' in a makey-uppy voice, because he says this is the excuse anyone gives when they're in trouble and have done something bad and don't want to take the blame for it. Harsh, but that's a Quinn Family Barney for you: it's v v rough-and-tumble and not for the faint-hearted.

If Dad knows he's about to introduce a word into my vocabulary, he'll raise his eyes as if to say, 'Here's a new one for you.' Other times when I look puzzled or plain ask out loud, 'What does that mean?' he goes, 'Look it up,' and I do. For example, he called me a 'refusenik' once and I was thrilled (even just for the way it sounds) and, although it has a historical reason for existing,‡ it really does do exactly what it says in the word.

I also like to say 'je refuse'⁶ to whoever asks me to do something I don't intend to do = all variations of refusing are v handy.

‡ Look it up, you'll thank me for it!

⁶ You see? It sounds much better spoken in le français. . .

45

Tonight Dad announces we will have Pasta à la Doug (which is his name). Anything 'à la Doug' will be an adventure in cuisine. I'm beginning to worry about what might be lurking in the fridge.

'Fusion cuisine,' Dad adds, and this does nothing to calm me. It's just another way of saying 'eclectic' as far as I'm concerned and means only that he's going to MAKE some food elements mix whether they like it or not, whether we like it or not.

All right, to be fair, it'll be edible (which is more than most of Gran's concoctions), but it might not be ideal as a taste sensation. I really have to learn to cook properly and not just rely on my pizza and salad combo. Mind you, Dad does a mean cheese-and-onion omelette that I adore, so here's hoping he can't find any pasta and goes back to his classic, signature dish.§

Then Harry, who has been attached to our mum's chest, falls asleep and his little head falls back. Mum is clearly also snoozing and doesn't notice. There is nothing to stop it and suddenly a spurt of boob milk shoots across the kitchen. It is horribly awesome. I am

§ Partic if it's accompanied by chips = NOM!

46

Mum's the Word

MORTO and *so* relieved that there are none but family members here to see this oh-so-natural-and-utterly-embarrassing incident.

Dad thinks it's *hilair* and laughs gustily.**

Dermot catches my eye. 'Jen, a word,' he says.

Uh-oh.

** **Adults are weirdoids = FACT.**

47

MAD MEN

I'm racking my addled and worried brain as I follow my brother to our front room.* I can't think of what it is that I've done wrong (this time) and so I'm reluctant to trail Dermot, but I can't think of a good reason to thwart him with.

'Have a seat,' he says.

EEP, this must be a BIG transgression.†

'I've been talking with the guys and we're all agreed

* Gran likes to call it the 'lounge' and I suspect she thinks that makes it sound classier than it actually is - it's just where we watch the telly.

† Delighted as I am to be able to use this word, I am dreading what it means in real life, as in, WHAT HAVE I DONE?

that we'd like you to handle the fan mail we've been getting.'

'WHAT?' I squeak, louder than any squeak has any right to be.

Then a strange burbling starts to come out of me and whatever language it's in it's not English: 'Blempremfembem.'

'Great, so you'll do it?'

I nod vigorously and sort of hurt my neck. My head is buzzing and my mouth goes dry. On the plus side, it stops me burbling, but I don't think my heart is beating any more. Ah well, swings and roundabouts, as they say.

OK, let me explain what a big deal this is. *Teen Factor X* is *the* show on TV for teenagers to show themselves off. It's not just for singers, it's for people with all sorts of different talents. And it's amazing to see the diverse talents that Irish teenagers have, and what they are prepared to do to be on TV. Uggs confessed that he nearly entered him and Gypsy, so that Pudsey dog that won *Britain's Got Talent* has a lot to answer for. Gypsy does nothing but bark and run around like a hairy eejit and I don't see how Uggs could ever harness that into an act. Embarrassingly, I had thought that I might try out too, but it was a pants idea[‡] and I prefer not to think about it now *EVER*.

The heats for this year's *TFX* were held before Christmas to ramp up the tension and excitement ahead of the competitive live shows. Ten Guitars got through. Now, with all the acts selected, there'll be a series of three live shows with more and more contestants going home as it all progresses.

And I am now secretary to Ten Guitars! I think I might like to bump the title up to Executive Secretary, or Executive Personal Assistant, or some such, but I'm *way* too excited to decide on that now.

'We'll need our own Facebook page and all that,' he says. 'Think you could do that too?'

If I'm not careful, I may explode with delight or delirium. I try to calm my breathing down and seem all on top of things.

'Where and when do I start?' I ask.

'Now, I guess. Up to you how you go about it all.

---

‡ v v ultra-mega-uber-ginormously pants of an idea. And the conclusion I came to was that my singing talents are not meant for the stage. And I am MUCH happier that way!

We have a bag of mail waiting for us at the studio, so you can get that when we do our next live TV performance.'

I was longing to see the studio but didn't dare hope I would so soon, as there are so many in the group and the numbers of relations and well-wishers going along to the *Teen Factor X* filming are rationed. Now, I'm 'official' . . . maybe even 'Access All Areas'? EEEP! I hope I'll get a laminate that says that?

My breathing is going wonky again so I'm glad when Dad shouts, 'Dinner is served,' and Dermot heads for the kitchen. I sit with my head between my legs till the faintness passes, then stroll nonchalantly to the next room to join the Quinns for whatever 'à la Doug' is on offer this evening. Even if it's OK, I doubt I'll swallow the barest mouthful.

I'M IN CHARGE OF THE TEN GUITARS' FAN MAIL!!! I want to shout it from the rooftop for all to hear. Maybe ring a few bells while I'm at it. This is BIG NEWS – whoop!

'Lasagne à la Doug,' Dad announces and that's more good news, because it'll have been one that Mum made ages ago and froze.

I can't get my thoughts to slow down and it seems to be influencing my table manners.

'It's lovely to see you eat so heartily, Jen,' Dad says. 'The smacking sounds are perhaps less necessary.'

Cripes. I haven't paid much attention to the meal to be honest, what with the whirl in my head. It reminds me of the time I was waiting for the bus and listening to my iPod simultaneously and I let loose a gust of tummy wind and only afterwards realized the startled looks I got were because I'd made a big bum parp – I couldn't hear it over Rihanna blasting in my ears.

I have proved that gusto and relish have a sound, though, and that can't be too bad a thing, surely?

'Sorry,' I murmur. 'It's delish.'

'A compliment to some mighty fine vittles,' Dad says in his best cowboy voice.

'How are rehearsals going?' Mum asks Dermot.

'Good,' he answers. 'Although it's hard to get all ten people to agree on most things. We only did the try-outs for *Teen Factor X* as a joke, and now that we're through to the live TV shows, we have to take it seriously. It's a bit of a leap for some of the lads.'

'As long as you're enjoying it,' Mum says.

'Ah, yeah, we are,' Dermot says. 'So far.'

'And as long as you're all agreed to play the same thing at the same time,' Dad says.

'So far,' Dermot says again. 'It's kind of mad, really. Oh, and Jen is on board now to run the fan club.'

My heart goes all funny-juddery and my face boils.

'Well, to look after the correspondence,' I say, trying to play down my excitement in case it makes me look childish – I am a teenager now and have to start getting a cool attitude going.

'An auspicious start to the year,' Dad says and gives me the 'look that one up' eyes.[6]

'What's suspicious?' Mum asks. She's only half-hearing everything at the moment. We all laugh. She smiles wanly, shrugs and says, 'The baby ate my brain when he was inside.'

'It'll grow back,' Dad tells her.

6 I do and it means favourable or (kind of) a good omen.

PLANS

I bolt to my room as soon as I can and text the Gang my news.

Dixie is first to reply with: **gud opp 4 making dosh**

I don't quite know what she means about it being good for making money, but I'm prepared to let it slide – it's not like she's not going to tell me at some point, and maybe I'd prefer not to know till then.

Uggs sends: **totes gr8! Gud 4 u!**

I'm waiting for a text from Gyp – no joke, she has sent me messages in the past – don't know how or why, just the way she rolls! No contact, she's playing it casual? Fine: two can play that game . . .

I can't sleep, so I try to make a list of what I'll need

to do as Executive in Charge of Fan Base, which is my latest title . . . in my head at least . . .

I wonder if it'll be like reading someone's private mail? I don't agree with anyone even reading a text unless it's for them or they're allowed to read it by the owner of the phone. Privacy is precious and it's hard to come by in a family, as I know from being a member of an inquisitive one. The Quinns are a nosey bunch. Dixie's got even more brothers and sisters, more than any of the rest of the Gang, and she says it's a nightmare even *thinking* in her house, because there's always someone who knows what's going on in your head and uses that as a licence to interfere with your life even more than they might normally do, which is a lot anyhow.

Of course Dixie is big on privacy since Jason Fielding put her pic on Facebook. To be honest, although it was a strange photo from a *ridic* angle, it wasn't anything Oakdale hadn't seen before. She was always getting in clinches with him at the Youth Club. Still, he has breached some moral law in her head and that's all that matters to her now. She will bring the pain to him.

I decide to check out her Facebook page and see

that she has changed her status from 'It's complicated' to 'Single' as she said she would, and her latest message reads, 'New Year is New Love Year!' Oh dear . . .

Then I see an awful picture someone has posted of a poor bird stuck to the ground by a piece of discarded chewing gum, saying lots of them are fooled into thinking it's food and then die like this, stuck and starving and thirsting to death – it confirms my suspicions that chewing gum is not for me. Yes, it can mask a honky breath smell, BUT it only masks it for a while and the honky fink of breath is still there when the gum is gone, just with a bit of old mint added. I share the photo in case there's truth in it. Wotevs, I don't trust the stuff any more and the post might save a few creatures?

I can't sleep even more now, so I do what I do best, which is to make a list. I title it 'PLANS FOR FANS'. I'll put a dedicated mailbox at reception in our school, Oakdale High, so local people can get in touch that way. I'll set up a Ten Guitars Facebook page tomorrow – well, Uggs or Dixie will because they're better than me at all that malarkey. I wonder if I should do all of the replies using a particular coloured ink? A colour dedicated to Ten Guitars?

I hear Gran's poker pals leaving and I'll bet they're a bit bendy from wine, and some of them a lot poorer too. Gran loves these nights, she says, because of people 'trying out their poker faces and lying through their false teeth', according to her anyhow. The Beast mobility scooter is purring away, though only to cross the road to where Francie lives. I try not to listen to the goodbyes because I'm always left with the feeling that those oldsters *flirt* with one another, and that is something I cannot comprehend, nor do I want to = makes me all yucky-squirmy.

Gypsy is barking and I hear Mr Nightingale call her in and the oldies wishing her a goodnight, even though she's a dog and doesn't understand. Then again, I was half-expecting her to text me earlier, so I guess I'm as mad as the rest of them.

I tuck myself up in bed and try and try to sleep, but it just won't come. I turn on the light and do a bit of reading until my eyes are tired and itchy. Then I switch the light off and try to settle down again.

I remember Uggs telling me that Francie auditioned

all of the mobility scooters till he found his one true Beast. There's a bumpy-backed bridge over a disused bit of railway line on the way into the villagey bit of Oakdale (i.e. the shops)* and Francie ordered his test drive to happen one Friday, with each candidate getting a fifteen-minute slot. The main criterion was getting over the bridge and back again, then whether the scooter had enough 'poke' to speed up and get him out of trouble if he was on the run. I shizz you not. It makes me laugh a little out loud and that's embarrassing, even though I am alone.

Baby Harry gives a cry in my parents' room, then he shushes, so I know he's having one of his night feeds. If only next door's dog could be quieted so effectively, I think. I try to imagine a remote control to switch Gypsy off and it makes me smile. I wouldn't let it have an 'on' button, I decide. My smile widens although I am in the dark and there is no one to see it, and I wonder if it's like that thing, 'If a tree falls in the forest and no one is there, does it make a sound?'†

* or the Precinct, as Uggs loves to call it, grinning all the way, because of the non-cool nature of our Oakdale precinct.
† I think it does, by the way.

Plans

Or, is the light actually on in the fridge when the door is closed?‡

The wind is picking up and howling around the house. I snuggle under my duvet and feel safe and warm.

All is well in the world.

‡ Dunno - but doubt it . . . that would be a monumental waste of energy, surely, and make the fridge a mad machine and *exhausted.*

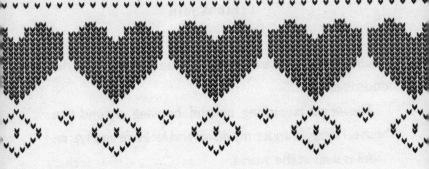

BEGIN AGAIN

The following day we're taking the decorations down and the house is looking ordinary again.

Mum seems overly devastated, which is v worrying to see.* Eventually she says, 'It's like we've stopped celebrating Harry's birth.'

Quick as a flash, Gran says, 'I'm sure the baby Jesus and *his* family felt just the same once upon a time.'

At least that makes Mum smile, even if it's in a grim way.

Worst of all, it's time for Dad to go back to work

---

* Hmm, is there something I should be doing about this? or would that make it worse?

and for us to go back to school. Getting back to normal feels like a kind of downer all right.

Don't get me wrong, I like school well enough, I just HATE our uniform (maroon,[†] says it all really) and some of my classmates are a pain. Oh, and the teachers are quite a sarky bunch, for the most part, although I'm guessing that's the way in schools all over the country.

But I'm Super Secretary to the hottest boy band in Dublin, so that's thrilltastic.

Even if it is sad to see some of the old fade away, or be removed, I tell myself there is much to be getting on with. We have new beginnings and a lot to do this year. I'm a tad exhausted even to think of how much. But it's exhausted in a good, tingly, excited way.

It's LASHING rain, though, like nature is downright angry about something and showing it, taking it out on the youth of Oakdale as we trudge back to school. We slosh through the *sheets* of water falling from the sky and gather in the main school hall, and I swear you can see the steam rising off us. We all smell a bit like wet wool too. I say this to the Gang and Uggs goes, 'Sheep, that's what we are,' and Dixie gives her best 'Baaa!'.

† It's the *noogack* of colours.

The headmaster addresses Assembly with New Year greetings that I can't quite believe he means because he forgets to smile. Then he congratulates Ten Guitars and Delia Thomas for making the cut on *Teen Factor X*, though he can't resist saying he hopes it won't distract anyone from their studies.

Delia is in our class and she does stand-up comedy and she's actually funny. This was a huge surprise to us because we didn't know she had routines and, more importantly, we all thought she was a bit of an oddball, v quiet and a nerdette. She's still all of those things but funny with it – who knew!

We go back to our familiar classroom and settle into learning stuff that may or may not be handy later in life. I never dis it since Dermot said I had supersaturated my cereal once at breakfast.

'You're just wasting the sugar,' he pointed out. 'There's too much in there and the excess is sinking to the bottom of the bowl. Supersaturation. Simples.'

He was right!

Dad was particularly impressed and went, 'Who said education is a waste?' I think he even gave Dermot extra pocket money for it. And that rankled. Blinkin'

hell, it wasn't like he'd won the Nobel Prize for science or anything. OK, I'll admit it, I couldn't think of anything as great to say to point up how much attention I was paying at school (and thereby craftily score some extra dosh), so I was a tad sore about the whole incident,[‡] if a little wiser after my bruv's info.

I also started using less sugar on my cereal, which is a healthier option all round.

‡ Hey, don't judge me. I'm only human.

MAKING DO

We're sitting in my room putting yarns together for our love-hearts project. If nothing else, it'll be a splendid way to use up any stray remnants left from other items – the ghost of gifts past,* if you will. It's recycling, at any rate, and therefore we're doing our v v small bit to save the planet.

'I may have to date a Guitar,' Dixie says.

The Gang is assembled ready to Knit 'n' Knatter, but this is not the opening gambit I was expecting from either of my chums.†

* I thank you!
† or Gypsy, who is an uninvited attendee and trying her best to sneak on to my bed* and get all comfy for a snooze.
* I have expressly forbidden this but she pays no heed.

'In what way date a guitar?' Uggs asks. 'Are we talking guitar object or Guitar a person?'

'A person, smartypants. Ordinary dating, Uggs, as in he takes me places and treats me like a princess.'

'But not the Guitar who is also my brother,' I check. I love Dixie, but that would be too complicated a relationship to add to our friendship.

'Dermot?' She squeals. 'That would be like going out with my own brother and so SO wrong.'

Phew – at least she still has SOME sense of right and wrong.

'I need someone high profile and they're all that and très cool. To be exact, they are *national* right now, what with *Teen Factor X* and all, and therefore just what I need.'

If she has her eye on Stevie Lee B, I may have to kill my bestest galpal.

'Gary O'Brien,' Dixie says. 'Discuss.'

Again, as if we need reminding, we should expect the unexpected with the Dixie, but Uggs can't help himself and he gives a honking snort.

'That would be Gary the Dork O'Brien?' he checks.

'Yes. That one. What other Gary O'Brien would I mean?'

'You can NOT be serious,' I say.

The Dork's initials are GOB and we usually use all forms of word associated with that to describe him, so we get into that now, hoping to end the temporary insanity that has consumed our friend.

'GOBdaw O'Brien,' Uggs says.

'GOB*dork*, even,' I add.

'Very funny, NOT,' Dixie says.

'There's Make 'n' Do and Making Do, Dix,' Uggs points out. 'I cannot stand by and allow the Dork Prince to enter your life like this.'

'It's verboten,' I agree.

Dixie sighs. 'I was going to allow my diet to wait until we got back into the swing of school proper, if it had to happen at all. Now it seems I'll have to bring the date forward, as I am not allowed the easy option of choosing the Guitar O'Brien, thereby avoiding the diet and any extra fluffing up because I could so score him right here and now. I am forced to go down the hard road of effort to regain my utter fabulosity.'

We know what that means: let the hunger begin. For all of us. My tummy actually rumbles at the notion.

'Surely he's a *leetle* funny?' Dix is not going to let up here.

'Funny in the wrong way, most of the time,' I say, as gently as I can.

'But a good guitar player?'

'Yes,' Uggs says.

And here's the thing: the Dork IS a good guitarist, and he's popular with the other guys too. He's just a bit, well, dorky. Or maybe he's just different; maybe I'm being mean? I hate it when things get all muzzy and grey in life. When things are a straightforward black or white, life is a lot easier, even if that's lazy too.[‡]

Dix lays a major one on: 'If I can't pursue the Dork, then I'll have to find an escort closer to home.' She fixes UGGS with a look. He gags as soon as I squeal.

'NOOOOO!' we go, in unison.

'That would be so wrong as to be even more wrong than a v wrong thing,' I say.

Dixie shrugs.

'This is a gentle gang, not a desperate dating agency,' Uggs points out – *states* as a fact, just so we can all be sure we know what we are here!

‡ or even wrong.

67

'Well, it was worth a try,' Dixie says. 'And if things don't go well for me datewise, you will both have to step up to help me save face.'

She shrugs as if her logic here is unassailable.

And I'm not sure how me stepping up to save her blushes is going to help. Does she mean I might have to go on a date with her? Surely that would confuse people, not least ourselves.

'I love you, Dix,' I say. 'But you're just not my type.'

I get a hard blow of a pillow for that.

I'm beginning to wonder if the Tongue did SUCH a bad thing. Can we not have him back?

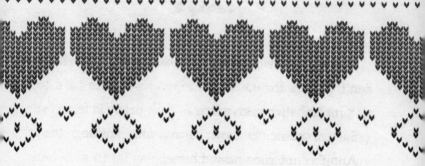

DARK ARTS

Dixie holds up some strands of wool. 'Bangles,' she says.

'Not from where I'm sitting,'* Uggs says.

'Not *yet*, you mean. I was thinking we should do some merchandising for the Guitars.'

'Like support bangles?' I venture.

'Yup. Though, as they might be expensive if we had to source rubber or plastic ones, I was wondering about making some with yarn.'

'Like a plaited friendship bracelet,' I say.

'Precisely. Though I think we should crochet the

---

* He seems to have acquired some 'tude during the festive break.

strands together in a chain stitch, to make them stand out from the crowd.'

'*Crochet?*' I whisper, partly in awe, partly in fear. 'I've only just come to basic terms with knitting, basic knitting. I am basic squared here.'

'We cannot sit still, Jen, we'll be left behind. We must embrace progress and the New. Do you have a crochet hook?'

I don't know why, but it's like the crochet hook is an instrument for the Dark Side in my mind and I try to put that nutty notion into words.

Dixie is quite kindly, which is a surprise: she's more of a tough-love gal. 'It's just that you don't know it yet and that's why you're fearful.'

'There is nothing to fear but fear itself,' Uggs says and we both go,

'Shut up, Uggs!'

'Noted,' he says.

'No.'

'No, what, Jen?'

'No, I don't have a crochet hook! I'm a knitter, and a knatterer, not a crocheteer!'

I think I may sound a scintilla hysterical. And I may

have made up a word there too. None of it takes away from the sincerity of my outburst.

'Uggs, go get chocolate-based snackerels and I'll nip home and get a hook. Then we'll get this new show on the road. You'll love it.'

Uggs gets to his feet and says, 'A change is as good as a rest,' and again gets another loud 'Shut up, Uggs!'.

For a quiet guy, he goes all soothsayer sometimes and it has to be stamped out toot sweet or he'll think he should spout wisdoms all day and get really boring.

I'm hoping Dixie returns with an actual crochet hook, as I think if it's a fishing one we are truly in trubbs.

As usual . . .

When she does come back she has Gypsy at her heels and she comes at us brandishing a newspaper like it's a weapon. Dixie, that is – Gypsy *is* a weapon.

'The pen is mightier than the sword,' she announces.

'And a lot easier to write with,' quips Uggs.

That's Eugene for you: he may not say a lot, but when he speaks it's sometimes worth listening to.

Dixie swipes the rolled-up newspaper at him and lands a nice swat upon his head. 'My lonely hearts is in,' she tells us.

71

This is not going the way anyone but Dixie has planned. She's now advertising herself in a newspaper[†] (which can only end in tears) and we're going to have to learn a new craft. I am, frankly, trepidatious.[‡]

'Check it out, *if you dare*,' she says.

'Might keep that treat until later,' I mutter. I *so* don't want to be implicated.

'Ditto,' says Uggs.

'Your loss,' Dixie assures us. 'Now, friendship bracelets. I'm thinking we should go with the colours of the hat you knit for Dermot, Jen.'

I rustle up what I have left of the two yarns, one black and one lime green, both cotton. They're a lovely combo, I think. I also did a little beanie for Harry and he looks just gorge in it.

Dixie chooses two strands of black and one of lime green, makes a starter stitch then chain stitches with the crochet hook till she has the required length, casts off and knots the two ends together. It looks

---

† Even if it is just our local schools' newspaper pretending to be a real newspaper.

‡ This may or may not be a word, I'll check later. Right now life is tense in the Jenny Q HQ.

really cool. And it has taken her hardly any time at all.

'We're in business,' she says. 'I'm thinking fifty cents per bracelet.'

'Fitty,' Uggs says.

'What?'

'Fitty Cent, that's what the rapper and his friends call him.'

'You are such a nerd,' Dixie tells him.

Uggs smiles, delighted with the accolade.

'I think they look a bit slim for the price.'

Dix considers this. 'OK.' She reaches for more yarn, crochets two more strands, then plaits them and, voilà, we have a decent product that's value for money.

'As long as the Guitars don't mind us making money off their success,' I point out.

'They'll be flattered,' Dixie insists. 'Besides, you're in charge of the fan club now, so you can tell them what's good for them.'

Uggs grins. 'And Dixie will tell you what's good for *you*, Jen,' he says.

Now *she* beams, all positivity. 'But of course, mes amis. And that will be good for all of us.'

Life is complicated and that's not 'maybe'.

I give a theatrical sigh and try to regain some space on my bed, but the terrier critter has taken up a goodly portion of the most comfy bit by the pillows. I try to shush her off, but she's lying like a big, heavy stone and refuses to budge. I give up, I really do.

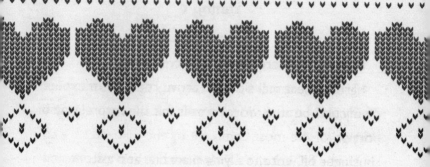

CONFESSION TIME

Well, this is just a mini confession, really, brought on by the introduction of the crochet hook and therefore an unease within me. I worry that I am set in my ways if I am resisting a new crafty option. And yet in other ways I am not myself. For example, I have begun to go a little nuts for Marmite. The reason I think this may be a bad thing (as in strange and worrisome) is that I have always been a devoted Kit Kat gal and therefore a lover of sweet things. In fact, it is true to say that the Kit Kat is the *Quinn-tessential* snack pour moi. Now, though, there are occasions when I'll opt for a rice cake smothered in the aforementioned *savoury* spread. It's not like me.

Are my taste buds changing in these teen years?

Is it a sign of creeping maturity?

If so, is there more of such activity that I must expect?

Should I be at all worried or is this the natural way of 'things'?

Maybe I'll write to a girly magazine and ask . . .

TELLY TUBBY

The weather is doing its best to wreck the New Year. Rain is still lashing down from the heavens and the temperature is freezing. Gran loves *weather*, i.e. talking about it in a doomy way, and she keeps muttering, 'We'll have snow.' Which would be pretty at least. The rain is plain grey and yuck.

Still, even floods cannot dampen the excitement of Ten Guitars and Delia Thomas appearing on television. The school is buzzing and I doubt many pupils are paying much attention in class, particularly the contestants themselves. I wonder what the buzz will be like if they make it to the final!

Mind you, *some* work is getting done – e.g. the fifth-year science boffins, also known as the science tragics, have installed an actually brilliant project in one of the hallways. They put sensors under some special pads on the floor and every time someone steps on them they use that energy to make some electricity. They are measuring how much energy we could harvest if we put the technology into public places or even our homes. The floor pads also light up = SO pretty (as well as practical) and I could spend hours standing in the corridor as people pass, watching the lovely lights in their random sequences. It's like a v useful disco. And, yes, *of course*, sometimes we kind of dance on the pads when there are no teachers around and that's good sport.

The 'mailbox' I put in reception is filling up with anonymous notes of goodwill for Ten Guitars, and a few nutty love letters that no one has had the guts to sign. It's v hard to read anything for Stevie Lee B, especially when it's telling him exactly how fit he is, because I feel that way about him too. And I don't want him thinking I might have written any of these. Some of them are v badly spelled, for one thing, and I would never let a letter go from me that wasn't well considered, with proper spelling and good grammar! And lots of nice, unusual words.*

Lack of names and addresses means I can't reply, even on behalf of the guys, so I just tell them that there's a range of greetings for them and they're more than welcome to read them. They're busy rehearsing, though, and few enough of them have the time to go through their mail. PHEW! I don't want SLB being snapped up from under my nose when his defences are down.

So the anonymous Randomers are not a threat, so far. The same cannot be said of the Slinkies. Samantha, Danielle and Emma Louise are sleek, older girls at Oakdale High and Sam is Dermot's girlfriend. But the other two are free range and available right now.

And always around.

Always.

They're also the same year as most of the Guitars, and certainly SLB, so they have ongoing access. It makes me squirm to think of all the time they get to spend with that guy, even if they are just looking at him and not talking to him and beguiling him.

* Then he'd guess straight away that it was me.

79

The only thing worse than big love is unrequited love, and that's what I have right here, right now.

Well, that and the problem of what to wear to the television studio this Saturday for the live show. I need something casually fab that doesn't make me look like a heap. If I get on TV, I don't want to look tubby, and apparently the camera adds four kilos or maybe more = *nightmare*.

'Dark colours, obviously,' Dixie says. 'V slimming and chic.'

'Well, I don't know,' I mutter. 'I mean, our uniform is maroon, which is a dark colour, and it's hideous, and even skinny minnies look dumpy in it.'[†]

'Point taken,' Dixie says. 'And well made too, Jen. Yes, our uniform is a crime against students.'

'And I don't have an LBD because I'm thirteen and that's not allowed, sexy-wise.'

'I'm thinking your navy-blue tunic with the Peter Pan collar.'

'Won't I just look like a kid, though?'

---

† The Slinkies only just about get away with looking human in the Oakdale High garb, and they're urban goddesses.

'No. You'll look funky and cute.'

'Hmm. But not fanciable.'

'The most fanciable thing will be you doing your job efficiently, looking after the guys. That's the biggest attraction of all. Plus you gotta be totes cool and professional.'

I really want to believe her.

'You need to *handle* yourself, girl.'

'K . . .'

'And you'll need to do something mad with your hair,' she adds. 'Totallahfunkify the look, underscore it, complement and challenge it. Leave that to me.'

Uh-oh . . .

DA BLUES

I guess when you get all excited and happy about something (anything) the universe feels the need to balance things out by delivering some shizz. But what in the name of fugly did we do to deserve the unravelling that's just occurring for the Quinns?

Mum is still like a friendly zombie in pyjamas wafting round the house. Gran does her best to get her to change into day wear, or at least take a shower, and Mum just gives her a big, vacant smile most of the time. She hardly says a word either, these days, and that's worrying. I've even tried to tempt her into singing silly words to songs, like we used to, but she's too far gone to take part properly. I hope Dad's right and her brain does grow back. I have been monitoring the situation and think maybe it is just a case of leave well enough alone and everything will work out. E.g. it can't be the first time this has happened to a woman, so therefore it will right itself. Hope so . . . But I do miss my mum.

The weather is still woejus, belting rain and driving winds. This afternoon I arrive in from school squelching and sodden and have to dash straight upstairs to get changed into dry civvies that aren't maroon.* There's a trail of wet footprints on the stairs when I'm done.

The first surprise in the kitchen is that Dad is home early. He doesn't look too happy about it, which is odd, because everyone likes time off work, surely? Unless they're a workaholic pervoid. Also, the conversation stops when I enter, and that can't be a good sign either. I wonder if I'm in trouble for something I may or may not have done.

'Is Dermot with you?' Dad asks.

Bizarro – I mean, why would he be? 'Er, *no*,' I say.

---

* Again, I have to ask, is any colour more rancid? Answer: I think not.

'Less of the attitude, thank you, Jennifer.'

Jeeps, Dad never talks to me like that. Someone sure ticked him off good earlier in the day if he's in this kind of mood.

'We'll need a family powwow later,' he tells me.

I so dislike the sound of that. What's going on?

'Mum?'

'Nothing to be afraid of,' she says.

And that does make me scared. Even the mention of nothing to be afraid of means there most likely *is* something to be afraid of!

Kit Kat and a quick skedaddle out of the line of fire for Jenny Q.

Dermot knocks on my door later and sticks his head round. The very fact that he knocked is not a good omen. Where does he get off being all polite suddenly?

'What's with the long faces on the parent types and Gran?' he asks.

I shrug. 'Search me. I don't like it, though.'

'You and me both, sister.'

Dad makes his awesome cheese-and-onion omelette for supper, but it doesn't taste quite as good as usual because of the atmos at the table. Even the crispy, skinny chips don't help = bizarreballs.

Finally, he gets to the point and reveals the reason for all the serious solemnity.

'I've been made part-time at the advertising agency and there's a chance I'll be made fully redundant if this recession doesn't lift sharpish.'

Cripes! I sure didn't see that coming.

'Times will be tough and we'll have to tighten our belts and all that. Sorry.'

'You have nothing to be sorry for, Douglas,' Gran says. 'You've always done your best.'

I feel all choked up. No wonder Mum's been acting oddly. No wonder Dad snapped at me earlier.

My heart could break for them, for all of us. And poor Mum, especially, should only have to worry about growing her brain back and looking after baby Harry, and not the fact that we are potentially headed for poverty.

Jeeps, maybe Dad will have to go on the dole and get charity butter vouchers.

'This is where we have to pull together as a family,' he says.

We all nod, but no one looks like they have a magical solution to our new and awful problem or even something comforting to say.

And just what did we do to deserve this?

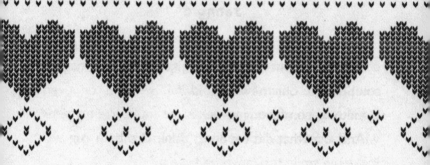

BUDGET

My fave duvet cover has died = sad face. It's been shredding and going threadbare at an alarming rate and has to be retired from active service as bed linen. However, now we're on an austerity* drive in the house, so I have decided to reinvent it, or recycle it, or up-cycle, or wotevs we're calling it this year. It's a fab blue-and-white striped material. I'm going to cut it into strips and tie them together, then knit it all on big needles into a tufty rag rug that I think will look great in the bathroom. In other words, I shall transform it through the magic of knitting. Eyethangewe! Recycling

* which is a serious-sounding word for major money-saving.

and saving the planet *and* making something pretty (and free) for the Quinn household.

I like when something makes me smile, like my pens with the feathery tops, and I think this bath rug will make me smile too, anytime I see it.

I tell Mum my plan and she barely acknowledges it. I am a little crushed, to be honest, and I am starting to feel like a neglected child right now. I thought she would be pleased with my initiative – old Mum would have been. But then she has not been like old Mum for a while now . . . However, I daren't complain, because we're all supposed to be putting our best foot forward and other cliches and so ons.

I'm in my room with Dix and Uggs and they think my rug plan is gentle genius – or at least they don't trash it in any way as an idea, so I take that as v affirmative.

I decide that while I am thusly ahead this may be an excellent time to wonder about some wonderment that I've been doing. I hold up a wooden knitting needle.

'Do you think this would be much good for doing away with a vampire?'[†] I ask.

† Vampires and teenagers seem to go hand in hand these days, especially in novels or the movies.

Budget

'Well, it is a pointy wooden stick,' Dixie says. 'The bigger sizes would do as stakes.'

'I think they're pretty much banned on aeroplanes, though,' Uggs offers.

'So I'd be defenceless on a plane?'

'Against a vampire, yeah, though I think they're more inclined to travel big distances in their coffins, with a bit of earth from their native country in them. And coffins aren't all that allowed on planes between Britain and Ireland these days, I think.'

'Safe enough on a flight, then,' I say, 'though the ferry might be a problem.'

'Best stay put,' Uggs advises. 'And keep the stakes handy . . . '

'Not that we'll ever be going anywhere ever again,' I say.

'Yeah, totes bummer about your dad's job,' Dixie says.

'I worry that we'll switch to budget biscuits when the latest batch of Kit Kats runs out.'

We all shudder for me. There is a real horror waiting to happen, trivial to those foolish enough not to know the worth of proper snacks and their place in teen development.

'Could be good for our healthy-eating kick, though,' Dixie says.

Even the mention of healthy eating makes me ravenous. Not that we've done anything about Dixie's regime yet, it's still TBA.

'Dad says it'll give him a chance to try things he should have done years ago,' I tell them. 'I dread to think what. He'll probably want to go back to taking embarrassing photographs of his family and showing them in public. He says it's art.'

Dixie sighs an understanding sigh and says, 'Tell me about it.'

I so don't want to deal with her Facebook débâcle and I could kick myself for sailing so close to the subject. I am saved by the most unlikely of saviours, i.e. Dixie herself.

'Apropos of vampires,' she says, 'may I remind everyone that Kristen Stewart of the *Twilight* series is a knitter?'

'How exactly do you know?' Uggs asks.

I wanted to ask that question, because it's not above Dixie to make something up and say it so often that it becomes real, especially for her.

Budget

'I read it,' she says, in a tone that suggests, 'Don't question the bingo master.'

'Where?'[‡]

'Where, what?'

'Where did you read it?'

'In a magazine, where else?'

'A Glossy?'

'Of course, a Glossy!'

'Must be true so,' he mutters.

Uggs has sisters, so he really *really* should know better than to goad a gal like this.

'Eugene,[6] do not cross me on this. It will end badly . . . for you.'

'For all of us,' I say.

Weirdly, at that moment it occurs to me that Gypsy would be an ally in the room – I must be going MAD. This is what happens to me in extreme circumstances:

‡ Yup, he had to go there.

6 Wotevah about anyone else calling him by his full name while angry, when Dixie does it he is in BIG doodah shizz and we all know it - smelly shizz stuff that sticks in the grooves of your trainer soles and follows you around sort of doodah . . .

I lose my moral compass and wish for bonkers things like that dog's presence.

'Ding ding,' I say. 'Time out!'

Uggs has started playing rugby with the school team and I wonder if that's making him all plucky and macho. It means he's hanging out slightly less with us, as he has to do practice two afternoons a week after school. I miss him then, but it's understandable that if he's got some sporting talent he should follow it.

It's rough stuff. Our wannabe class bully, Mike Hussy, plays. He's a beefy lump and he's a big part of team scrummages, basically using his brawn to push other lads around. He loves flinging himself on other players too, as violently as possible, and forcing them into the ground. Rugby suits him and his aggression.

I asked Uggs if he was worried about ending up with cauliflower ears and a crooked nose.

'Nah. I'm fast, Jen,' he explained. 'I grab the ball and run like the wind. Can't be caught. Thusly, I'll stay pretty.'

I hope he's right. It all looks like rough anarchy to me. Plus it is v v mucky during these dismal, dark winter months. And so *cold*. The one match Dixie and I attended, it was so freezing it looked like the players were following their breath around the pitch. I'm all for exercise as long as it's indoors, which is why I like playing volleyball in the school hall. Also, it doesn't have too much bodily contact.§ Rugby, on the other hand, is a game full of lads throwing themselves roughly on other lads and burying them in the mud under a mountain of bodies. And pushing and shouting. Way too dangerous for any sensible and sensitive creature, like yours truly.**

§ Hockey does, and involves sticks = *WEAPONS* and I therefore avoid it at all costs.

** Me!

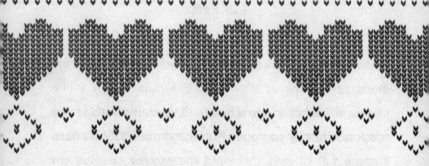

PEN PALS

I feel a bit mean doing all the fan stuff for Ten Guitars but nothing to help Delia Thomas. She is a *Teen Factor X* contestant too, and she's in my class, and a pal. Well, a pal in as much as the Gang hangs around a bit with her and a new girl called Maya, though not much at home, because the Gang has known one another since we were kiddy small and newcomers just wouldn't fit so well into that arrangement.

She hasn't actually asked for help, so maybe she doesn't need any. Still, I find myself asking if she'd like me to set up a mailbox for her too, and she says, 'Why not?' though I can't judge whether she thinks it's a good idea or not.

'I doubt anyone will be interested in writing to me,' she says.

Again, I can't gauge whether she thinks this is the truth or she's playing up some false modesty. She's hard to read.

'Oh, I'm sure people will get in touch,' Uggs says. 'I loved your routine on TV, and those glasses were cool.'

Actually, Delia made the front of the free schools' local paper* over Ten Guitars, with a photo of her from *Teen Factor X* and the title 'Spexy Lady!'.

Uggs is nattering away now and he seems v chummy with Delia and Maya. They're laughing at whatever he just said, which I missed because I was away in my head remembering the newspaper story. I have missed a vital element of the convo and now I'll never catch up.

I suddenly notice that Uggs is a lot taller than me. When did that happen? And his voice sounds a little bit deeper, though maybe he's putting that on to impress the girls. And OMG that's another thing – he's *flirting* with them!

I look around for Dixie to share my observations, but she's further along the corridor giggling at

* In which Dix is now on the love-hunt.

something Gary the Dork O'Brien is saying. She's also being a little too loud, like she's trying too hard to be noticed having a *super* time.

My Bestests are losing their marbles. But then, my whole world seems to be going a bit skew-whiff, so why should this area be left behind in the mad mêlée?

I begin to wonder what would happen if Dixie and Uggs got 'significant others'. I mean it's going to happen some time (I guess?). We're not *entirely* awful, or are we? There must be some hope that we'll grow into decent human beings, even if we're a bit unfinished now. But if they pair off with other people, I'll be alone. Solo. Because, let's face it, the chances of me scoring Stevie Lee are minimal.[†] And as I don't have any feelings for anyone else in that way, it would just be me, by myself, whenever the others were on dates and so on.

I am not a jealous kind of person, I don't think, but, as you'll have noticed, I am a bit exclusive about Dixie and me and Uggs as a Gang. We've been together for ever and, even though we have other friends, they're

† If not less . . .

the only ones I want sitting in my room chatting and knitting with.[‡] No one could ever be as special to me as they are. I can't bear the thought of being without them or of a big change happening between us: it spooks me. I have to get busy before I get low about it all. I go ahead with the Delia Thomas box and place it next to the Guitars' one. And I am downright glad to hear the bell ring for classes to begin.

As we make our way to the classroom, Dixie parts company with the Dork, who's in a higher class, like the older man she has advertised for.

'What was the hyena routine for?' I ask, when she catches up with me. 'There's no way the Dork was that funny.'

'Ooh, get you,' is her unfantabulous retort.

This does nothing to improve my day. I am in no mood to be teased. I actually give a low growl.

'For your info, Miss Snippety Snip, Gary[6] is a bit of a sweetheart. Obviously he has style issues, but he's a guy and that sort of drawback afflicts them. It can be

‡ Again, I stress that Gypsy does *not* count.

6 She is surely only three breaths away from calling him Gaz . . . tragic!

97

worked on. And he is steeped in coolmost from being an Actual *Guitar*.'

'He is an *Actual Geek*,' I remind her.

Sometimes I think I should charge money for having to point out the glaringly obvious to people, especially those who have gone mental, like Dixie.

'Do you think everyone saw?' she asks.

'Oh yes, everyone saw and everyone heard and everyone was shocked, frankly.'

'Great.'

Again, I give up: truly, honestly, deeply, I do.

SUPER SATURDAY

I'm spending the whole of Saturday at the television studio with Ten Guitars. That way I can deal with any fan-based issues. It's SO totes awesome that I can't sleep a wink. Well, who could? A person made of stone, maybe, but not the flesh-and-blood wreck that is presently masquerading as Jenny Q. Maybe I'm getting like my mum, who is now a less substantial replica of her former self.*

We are leaving v early, as we have to be at the studio at 8.30 a.m., so I reckon I am safe from Dixie's style plans. But, oh, how wrong I am. At

* Which is, actually, not a laughing matter but something I cannot address today, on the first live show of *TFX*. EEP!

7 a.m. Dixie is at the door with all sorts of hair paraphernalia.

'Stylist to the stars,' Dad says, and Dixie goes all giggly. He has an effect on her that I just do not understand. The guy is *old* and he's, er, *my dad*, so everything about this situation is unacceptable. She calls him DOUG,[†] for freaksake!

She is briefly distracted by coffee and toast, then it's down to business. Dixie hauls me up the stairs to my room and plonks me on the stool in front of my make-up table/vanity-type place/desk with a mirror above it thingy. I look at it with new eyes and finally realize what a dangerous situation I'm in. What if Dixie decides she wants to apply some make-up too? It's so early still and there are so many pens and pencils on my desk/vanity 'unit' that she could reach out, grab a marker (permanent or non-permo, doesn't matter in this scenario) and then *she'll mark me up like a clown.*

'I have decided that you need to make the most of your curls,' she says.

I normally try to straighten out the rampant kink in

† Yes, that is his name, but OMG she should Not. Go. There.

my hair and it takes time, effort and quite a lot of product.[‡]

'I'm guessing objections are futile,' I squeak.

'Totes.'

'Urp!'

She takes out a diffuser, attaches it to the hairdryer and we're off. I cannot bear to look in the mirror while it's all happening before my eyes so I keep them shut. She fluffs and primps and sighs and then goes, 'Ta dah!' so it's time to check out the carnage.

Strange to relate, the result is quite nice. My hair looks soft and shiny and the curls are cute.[6]

'Let's do a fluffski, spray, then pop on your nice navy headband with the flowers. A slick of lip gloss is all you need make-up-wise at this hour. And when you get out of those *hid.eee.us* pyjamas and into your nice *gúna*,[§] we are READY.'

[‡] Eeek! I have just realized that in our new straitened circumstances I'll have to stump up the dosh for hair stuff, stuff I think is *essential* but which other mortals may think is folderol - *not good* . . .

[6] Funky cute but not kiddy cute.

[§] Gúna is the Irish word for 'dress' and is pronounced 'goona' - sounds great, doesn't it!

I struggle into my clothage, trying not to muzz up my 'do, and when I am 'prête' (according to Dixie), she sprays me liberally with dewberry eau-de-something and says, 'Not bad, actually. Will *do*.'

I look, well, OK = hooray!

'I am rageballs I'm not going,' Dix tells me. 'I could *so* use this day to get a fabulous significant other.'

'Le sigh,' I say, nodding in support.

'Full textage throughout the proceedings and a debrief tomoz, yeah?'

'Totes.'

'And remember: I'll be watching it live on TV, so I'll know if you're ignoring me, or even lying.'

'I hear you.'

'Good. Plus I know where you live and I can hunt you down if I have to. You know I can.'

'I do.' (And I do! I so do!)

'All correcto, so. I'm off back to bed. Laters.'

'Tayters.'

You might have thought that was the end of pals at this hour, but you would be wrong. We go downstairs just as Uggs and Gypsy arrive.

'We wanted to wish everyone good luck and all that.'

Gypsy barks and does a funny little running-around-in-circles thing.

'She loves the look,' Uggs tells me.

'Dixie Purvis to the rescue,' Dix declares, with a martyred face that says she had to give it her ALL.

'Er, hello, I didn't think I was that much of a heap,' I say.

Gypsy barks, Uggs tries to say, 'You're not,' and Dermot comes barrelling out with, 'We'll be left behind if we don't get our sorry butts to the school PRONTO.'

I check I have all I need (a large bag of pens, stationery and phone) and CHECK/TICK all is there.

'Jen, where's my guitar?' Dermot wants to know.

'Wherever you left it last,' I say factually.

'Sheesh, *attitude*,' he says. 'At this hour?'

He raises his eyes to heaven and my Bestests nod in sympathy. WHAT??? He is the one being El Divo, not me. My job is Fan Club Liaison Officer, not skivvy to the star.

We go into the kitchen in search of the errant instrument, without which, let's face it, Ten Guitars will be less than ten.

Mum is nursing Harry at the table. She takes one look at me and bursts into tears. Jeepers, that bad!

Dad says, 'Jen, you look really lovely.'

'Nice try, but clearly not,' I say, indicating Mum as my proof.

I'm only hoping Harry doesn't pick up on her *palpable* horror at my appearance, because him crying will break/shred us.**

'No, no, Jen,' Mum blubbers. 'I'm just so *happy*!'

Er, right. That would be why you just started crying? This is definitely turning into something to worry over. It's not even 8 a.m. and already I am WRECKED.

** And it's v v penetrating as a sound too . . .

SAVAGE SATURDAY

Dad drives* us to Oakdale High School, Place of Dreams,† and our rendezvous for the transport to the show venue. A little crowd of well-wishers has gathered to see the band off, and I find that madly touching. I feel myself well up a bit, so maybe I can understand Mum crying because she's happy,‡ strange as that is.

Gary O'Brien is fist-bumping friends and fans alike and generally grinning from ear to dorky ear. Most of

* The weather is fierce still.
† I know sarcasm is supposed to be the lowest form of wit, but sometimes it works and, besides, there's a lot of it at Oakdale, courtesy of the many jaded teachers we have.
‡ Maybe??

the group seems to be assembled, which is a relief: keeping track of ten adolescent guys is a specific kind of chore. Stevie Lee is lurking in a doorway chatting with the Slinkies, so my heart sinks a tad at that. He sees us arrive and waves, though it's probably to Dermot and not me. I smile anyhow, then try to look all efficient. They start to make their way over.

'Good luck,' Dad says. 'Break a leg, but not any guitar strings.'

Dermot gives him a wan grin for his efforts at humour.

'We'll be glued to it and we'll record it for you to watch later. And, of course, we'll be voting early and often.'

Oooh, this is it. I've got to get out and into the elements and I am not looking forward to what the rain may do to my hair. It tends to fuzzy it up and, today of all days, I don't want to look like a dandelion head (seeds or flower) now that my head is au naturel . . .

I put up my transparent umbrella[6] and it captures the wind and drags me to the bus.

6 ✓ like the ones the Queen of England uses, though she has a range with different trims to match different outfits and I just have pink.

Savage Saturday

There is a stern woman with a clipboard trying her best to marshal everyone on board. Just as we're about to get on, Samantha Slinky throws herself at Dermot, smothering him in kisses for luck. You'd think he was off to war, not a talent show! Although I suppose it is our very own Star Wars? Anyhow, it's well embarrassimundo. Even Dermot looks askance.§

The Slinkies give SLB pecks on the cheek and he gets on the bus and passes by to go and sit towards the back. At my seat he leans over and says:

'Mmm, you smell great. Don't know whether to breathe in or take a little nibble out of you.' Then he flashes his legendary smile and I am sure I'll faint. I reach for my bag on the floor, which is really an opportunity to get my head between my legs in the recovery position and breathe steadily till the dizziness passes.

The passengers are quite quiet, just chatting among themselves. There's a slight air of apprehension, I think. The bus is buffeted by wind, and the swish of the tyres on the rain-sodden road and the windscreen wipers working fast are the main

§ WHAT a word!!

sounds inside the bus. Out of nowhere Gary O'Brien plonks himself beside me.

'Sister Jen!' is his greeting.

Suddenly I feel that my dress might be nun-like, thus provoking his outburst, and I get agitated.

'Gary,' I acknowledge (for it is he).

'Looking forward to the day?'

'Yeah. You?'

'Affirmative. Though I'm nervy too. Hope I don't faint like that little girl did during the Dublin tryouts.'

My heart freezes over. Everything goes into slow motion. The air is sucked out of the bus. A red-alert ringing noise fills my head. I cannot breathe. My face boils.

I was that 'little girl'!!!

I have been blocking the memory from my mind, but now that it's back, my life is over. It dawns on me things are worse than I ever could have imagined – WHAT IF SOMEONE WORKING ON THE SHOW RECOGNIZES ME? This situation could SO not be worse even if it tried. I'm hyperventilating now, though trying to cover it up as a mild cough. My heart is banging so hard against my ribs it feels like it will burst out through them.

Here's what happened. I wanted to try out, singing, for *Teen Factor X*. I didn't tell the Gang till it was v late on (to avoid mockery) and there was tension over that. No one else knew of my (stupid) plan. On the day of the auditions I got overwhelmed and fainted as I walked through the door to the judges' room, but it wasn't shown clearly on TV because Dixie came to my rescue and forbade the use of the footage. BUT they showed enough for the country to know someone had keeled over . . . ME!!!

How could I not have thought of the consequences further along in time? Turning up with the lads today puts me directly in line to be seen and recognized. There are no words to cover the horror. This is *by far* the worst thing that has ever happened to me. It is a **CATASTROPHE!**

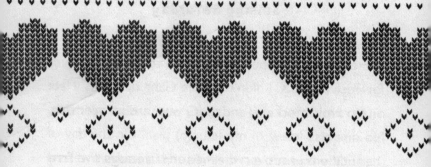

SINKING SATURDAY

There are photographers flashing cameras at the Guitars as they disembark from the bus at the venue, a place I am fast wanting to call the TERMINUS, as it may be the END of my life, career, breathing, etc. I'm clearly not a member of the group so no one is interested in taking my picture.* I am careful to keep my head down all the same. Now I wish my umbrella wasn't see-through but made of the thickest, darkest material ever to hide me from the world entirely. I can feel tears bubbling up in my eyes, but I'm hoping that it looks like the rain has wet my face. It's like I'm drowning, though I am walking on the ground. I have never felt so bad. My

* MEGA-ULTRA PHEW!

heart is in bits. I wish Uggs and Dixie were here. Even Gypsy would do.[†]

As there is no alternative JQ plan, I text my mates for support.

ME: **V v bad here = wot if sum1 recogs me frm wen I fainted in trials?!?!**

Their replies explain a lot about them both, as people and pals . . .

DIXIE: **is poss bt jst deny**

UGGS: **nah, wont hap, relax, enjoy!**

ME: **mite die of stress . . .**

DIXIE: **u probly wont, fear not**

UGGS: **DON'T!**

DIXIE: **am I missing much hottie action?**

A girl with dyed, deep-red hair is allocated to us as a group.

'Oh, hi!' she says in greeting. 'Another red head. Great! I'm Mel.' She has a lovely smile.

'Jenny,' I say, patting my hair (a lil) self-consciously. 'I'm looking after the fan side of things for the band.'

'FABringtons. I've got lots to offload on you. PeeLENTy to keep you occupied.'

† Extreme, I know, but things are v bad indeed.

I'm glad to hear it. I need to hide and stay v v busy. I also really like Mel, immediately. It's like she accepts me, no questions, and that's good.

'I'm a runner here at the show, which basically means I really do run around a lot doing things for people, usually what they don't want to do themselves, so if something goes wrong, I get the blame too.' She laughs at this and it's a nice, musical sound.

She gathers the Guitars and leads them to a big dressing room.

'Guys, this is yours for the day. It's the one Jedward use when they do a gig here. And One Direction are next in, after you, when they do their Dublin gig. I have ID for you all. I'd appreciate it if you try to stay together, because there'll be a lot of travel over and back to the stage area for rehearsals and so on. We're on a strict timetable, so there's no leeway for getting lost or going missing. Time is precious.'

The lads are only just about paying attention, because all along the length of one wall is a table groaning with food. Cereals, fruit, croissants and Danish pastries = bliss! They are all drawn to the feast and, as long as the table is laden all day, the show organizers will have no problem keeping them together and in one place. The way to manipulate these guys is deffo through their stomachs.

'That girl is seriously *hot*,' one of the Guitars is reporting to another, surreptitiously.

'Serio-ly true.'

'Believe, bro,' GOB says, as he stuffs his gob.

Mel is a hit. I want to be her, no doubt about that. She has a 'look' and is chic and cool and a role model/icon-type. Girl crush, even. The Slinkies look like country cousins by comparison.[‡]

So what's she got? Well, a v cool nose stud for starters – not EVEN a stud but a lil diamond. Now, it has to be said that she's at LEAST twenty-one, so she's old, but she can still carry funky. Her gear is all sparkly, with a colourful 1950s-style petticoat lifting out her skirt above some groovy fishnet tights. She's wearing purple Doc Martens, so RESPECT and wow! Her pens are all stuck in her hair. Her nails are painted a v dark red and her lippy matches them. I feel prissy and a frump beside

---

[‡] All due respect to all country cousins there (especially mine), just employing a lazy phrase, I guess - must look up where it came from to cover my sorry butt.

her. I am in neat little pumps, thick tights and my dress has a collar, for frippsake. I am Miss Prim, Miss Proper.

Best of all things about Mel, if you ask me right now, is that she is NOT ME. So, I wouldn't mind being her, as a result. I'd love to be her now or any other time, TBH, due to her greatness.

Oh, and . . . Mel has a ring on every finger (including thumbs) and possibly bells on her toes![6] She shall have music wherever she goes, certainly today, with Ten Guitars in her charge.

She gets everyone's attention by saying, 'You're on first, by the way, because you're the most complicated act.'

BY THE WAY?! This is big news, not just BTW.

You could hear a pin drop in this room, then the actual sound of Gary actually dropping a bowl of Rice Krispies and going, 'SHIZZ! Milk everywhere, and it really honks when it goes off – sorry, guys.'

'Could be the edge we need,' Dermot mutters, drily, and I *have* to love my bro just then because it lifts me and I give an out-loud honk of laughter. I am glad he's here.

6 Hope so, anyhow.

114

Sinking Saturday

As it happens, Stevie Lee is on the other side of Dermot giving a nice, appreciative laugh too = not bad company to be in.

The Dork is now on all fours trying to clean up his mess. He seems to be collecting each Rice Krispie individually and putting it back into his bowl. He's going to be some time, so.

STEWDIO

It's *SO* hot in the auditorium, which is made into an impromptu studio for the day. The show will go out live on television tonight, so everything has been set up to suit that. There are blazing lights everywhere and no air coming in that I can detect. It's also *SO* exciting, though, so no one cares if they melt. The guys are introduced to everyone and I doubt if they remember even one name that's hurled at them. The presenter, Margo Frisby, is v v glam on TV, but right now she's in a tracksuit looking tired and hassled. Someone is obvs talking into her earpiece and she doesn't look v pleased with what she's hearing. I decide to sit in the audience seats for the rehearsal and it feels good to be able to hide away in the dark, safe.

I take a sneaky pic of Margo and send it to the Gang.

DIXIE: **URGH! Margo lukin ruff**

ME: **Yup. Gr8, eh?**

DIXIE: **v much so**

UGGS: **Margo has let herself go!**

ME: **tee hee**

Everything is stop-start with the Guitars' rehearsal so that the camera shots and sound levels can be decided. There is one brillo camera that swings around the ceiling of the auditorium and does circular shots, zooming in and out on the group. It's super for me to be able to gaze at Stevie Lee without looking like I'm staring. The camera just loves him. Weirdly, the Dork looks quite good on screen too.

It takes ages to get everything nailed down, but it's all so new and fascinating that it doesn't seem like a chore for any of the lads. They have to go through their song, painstakingly, with moves, because the sound department has so many of them to get a microphone on to. There's a small army from that department dashing about and sighing and throwing their hands in the air. I get the distinct impression that the camera people are enjoying all the hard work their colleagues have to do, and they all look like they have a tiny grin at the corner of their mouth. There is a floor manager marshalling everyone, and he is fascinating to watch and listen to. He looks v cool in his head-cans and a tiny mike round in front of his mouth to talk to the control room. I think that would be a job I'd like.

Mel plonks down beside me, taking a nanosecond out from her running. I float my theory that everyone is secretly enjoying the sound department's hassle and she grins widely.

'They love to fuss and they *are* being drama queens today, with such a big group, BUT they are also great at their jobs, so I'm pretty sure they enjoy showing that off too.'

When everyone is (nearly) satisfied that they have cracked the beast, they all go through the number again in one go and that's it, the Guitars are off and the next act is wheeled on. There'll be a full show dress rehearsal in the afternoon.

As we're on our way back to the dressing room a passing woman stops and gives me a long look. I recognize her from the tryouts and I am TERRIFIED she'll recognize me, so I keep my head down and try to hide behind Dermot. My legs are like concrete and my lungs seem paralysed = FEAR CENTRAL. The air in the building seems too thin now and I have to pant a bit to stay alive. The woman looks like her brain is throwing some sort of memory up to her to figure out, but (after what feels like several centuries) she eventually shakes her head and goes about her business. I am surprised I didn't just fall down with the terror of it. If I was sweaty from the heat in the studio, I am now drenched from horror and fright too.

'You're humming,'* Dermot says.

'All the music in the air,' I gasp.

He gives me the eyebrows-raised look that says he doesn't really believe me – he's my bro, so he knows what the humming means. He chooses not to 'go there', though, which is a v welcome megaphew for this small Jenny Q.

When faced with peril all beasts have two choices = fight or flight. I decide on the latter – well, flight into a quiet place out of that busy, dangerous corridor, so I will hide for the rest of the day in the dressing room at

---

* I hum when under pressure – actually, I hum a lot louder than I realize I'm humming when I'm under pressure.

a table and chair I fix up as a desk. Food and liquid are provided, so I have all of my basic needs (plus a great vantage point for more SLB watching).

I begin to sort out my pens and stationery and this calms me.

The lads strum together to keep supple and up to speed, after they've vacuumed up the rest of the breakfast buffet, that is.[†] Things are not as bad as they might be, so this will do for now.

Then a small crew of people comes through the door. They are making the behind-the-scenes videos that will be shown throughout the show. EEP! I sneak a quick look in my mirror to make sure I am not too shiny after the heat of the stage lights and the fright in the corridor. I look plausibly human, just about. The lads start goofing about for the camera.

Mel arrives with two bags of correspondence and a batch of photos of the band that were taken at their auditions. 'You can send these to the fans. And if you

[†] I make a note to fight for nourishment whenever food deliveries occur - these guys are like a swarm of locusts. I need my strength for the trials I am presently encountering, let alone whatever further test lies ahead.

leave the reply letters with me, I'll pop them into the company postbox.' She doesn't even acknowledge the crew as they film her delivery: too used to them by now, I'd say.

She sees the empty food table. 'Better get more supplies in for the troops.'

This band marches on its stomach all right, and she knows it. Food and plenty of it is also the way to the guys' hearts: they will be so in love with her by the end of the day.

I look at the bags and realize I came v underprepared. I have lots of pens‡ but just two pads for the replies. I'll be all day getting through this lot and I will certainly need everything Mel has provided.

'Guys,' I say, as loudly as I can. I'm still not heard over the din in the room. I clap my hands, then bang on my table. I finally get some attention. 'Could you all take a pen and sign the band photos, so I can get them out to your adoring public.'

There are whoops and laughs and everyone gets down to business.

It's only then I notice the camera pointing at me! I

‡ Natch. I'm JQ, after all, and I love writing and words.

121

am going to be on TV and I hope I won't mind this appearance on the show as much as my last one, when I so didn't want to be seen. I duck under the table all the same, rummaging in my bag, because I can do without any lingering shot of me being available for broadcast. I prefer a bit of anonymity just now.

FEVER

Within an hour, my head is swimming with the amount of 'I love you's I am having to read. Sometimes it's someone loving all ten guys, sometimes just 'lurvin' one. And it is v uncomfortable to see your own brother described as a sex god by a stranger, or the Dork being told he's a hottie by some crazy delusional.* Some have sent a photograph and mobile-phone number, begging for a meeting, always stressing that they are 'not mad' and have 'never felt like this about anyone ever before'. It's like there's a generation out there gripped by a fever: Ten Guitars fever. I simply put a

* Although I must remember that beauty is in the eye of the beholder, according to some ancient lore or other . . .

signed photo of the band into an envelope addressed to the devotee and seal it, ready for posting.[†]

Since I started, the lads have demolished the mid-morning snacks, crisps of all flavours, topped off with burgers and chips for lunch. The room is stuffy and smells of onions, cheese and wet socks. I finally realize what is odd about the place: there are no windows. It could be any time outside, though it's probably 2:30, like it says on the clock. I need to breathe fresher air, stretch my legs and 'powder my nose', so I slowly edge out of the door, scanning the corridor for the roving camera crew or, more importantly, anyone who might put two and two together re my disazzo try-out for the show and identify me.

All clear.

I scoot towards the ladies' loo and then THAT woman from earlier (in my life as well as the day) rounds the corner. Maybe even thinking of her has caused her to appear? She's reading something on her mobile, so I have *JUST* enough time to duck through

---

[†] I cannot sensibly deal with my own pash for Stevie Lee B, so how am I supposed to engage meaningfully with someone else's?

the nearest door before she catches sight of me. I stand, heaving with horror and lack of oxygen. Then a small voice says, 'Hi, are you with the show?'

I give an 'EEP!' and a bit of a jump as I turn around. It hadn't occurred to me that there'd be someone in here. Then again, I could be standing in a broom cupboard and it wouldn't surprise me — I just picked the nearest available escape without scoping it beforehand.

The voice belongs to a diminutive‡ fairy of a girl. She has blonde curls, huge blue eyes and a wide smile. I recognize her from the early rounds. She's from Cork and has a sing-song accent when she talks as well as when she sings.

'Er, kind of with the show,' I explain. 'I'm actually with Ten Guitars.'

'Oh my TFX! I LOVE them!'

'Well, I'm not in the group, cos I'm a girl and all that. And I can't play the guitar, so . . . But my brother is sort of one of the leaders. His name is Dermot. I'm Jenny.'

‡ Yup, it's a v good descriptive word and I'm delighted to get some proper use out of it! And, yes, she is v small and dainty.

125

'Great. I'm Jess. I'm one of the contestants.'

'And you *do* play guitar. I remember you from the tryouts.'

She laughs. 'Yeah. Just the one guitar, though.'

It suddenly dawns on me that Ten Guitars have an unfair advantage because there are, well, TEN of them, so they have lots of people voting for them. There's only one of Jess.

'I'll make sure to vote for you,' I tell her.

'Only if I'm good.'

'You so will be!'

Jess was fabtastico in her audition round. She sang a song she wrote herself about her first day at school. It was hilarious. And it made me glad that I hadn't got through – well, I hardly got through the blinkin' DOOR before I keeled over!

There is a knock on the door and I scurry behind it as it opens. I'm doing the 'I'm not here' signs to Jess and she grins. Then Mel hooks her face round the door.

'What are you up to?' she asks, laughing.

I shrug, oh so innocently. 'Just getting around, making friends, you know.' I even try a winning smile.

'I do,' she assures me, nodding. 'I *do*. Right, young Jess, time for your rehearsal.' She turns and gives me a quick, appraising look and says, 'I'll see you later.'

She knows I'm ducking and diving. I am useless at guile. Or even downright lying.

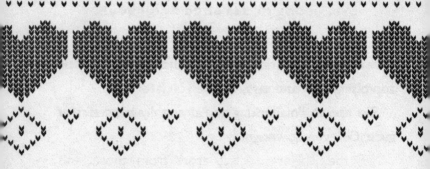

EVERYBODY NEEDS
GOOD NEIGHBOURS

I'm making my way back to Ten Guitars when I see a name I recognize on a door, and I decide to visit. Delia Thomas is sitting, chewing her nails, on a divan in her personal dressing room.

'Yo, Jen,' she says. 'Wotchoodoin' here?'

'Ten Guitars' stuff,' I say, like that's a given, or natural, or not unusual at least.

'If they don't get to me soon I'll have gnawed my hand off,' she tells me. 'My nerves are in BITS!'

'You have no need to worry,' I say. 'You're just great and SO funny.'

'Oh, come on, Jen, have you seen the line-up? The

other acts are fantastic . . . well, maybe not the guy on banjo with the dancing cousins . . . '

'Or the contortionist who can't really bend all that far back?'

'OR the juggler . . . But apart from those, this competition is HOT.'

'And so are you.'

Janey Mac, though, I'm like Therapist to the Stars today – pep-talking everyone, fluffing them up to go out there and do their level best or, preferably, even better than that. Exhausting . . . but so flippin' exciting!*

I wonder if my role in life is as a wing-person type, or an agent, or manager, or general positivity sayer? A life coach, peut-être? Which would be great if I knew anything at all about life, other than that if shizz can happen, it will.†

Delia pops her hand back into her mouth and gnaws again, wincing with how close she is getting to the quick of her nails. I can nearly feel the hurt of it myself. She'll

* When I'm not worrying about being revealed as the fainting failure of the Dublin tryouts.

† Which is probably not a bad start . . . the only way is up and all that?

129

start on the skin around her nails soon and then have very sore, stumpy fingers for weeks.

'Do you wanna come hang with the lads?' I ask.

'Nah, I'm next up. Last up, actually. They're keeping the "funny" till last. Thanks for the offer, though.'

'Well, when you're done, we're number eleven down the corridor. It's v v smelly and full of boys and now devoid of food, but you're welcome.'

'Yeah, I might. I'm crappy company at the moment, though, so they may not be that thrilled to see me. And I'm so not feeling the funny today, either, which is dire.'

'Do what you normally do and you'll have them rolling in the aisles.'

'You're looking very . . . '

' . . . prim?' I say.

'No, reliable. Trustworthy.'

I *guess* that's good?

I hurry along to the band's room thinking how glad I am that I didn't make it on to the show. I don't think I could handle the stress. The worry of being identified as the (Capital Failure) fainter is bad enough, so I'd probably fall apart completely if I actually had to perform too. But at least I get to be a (helpful) part of the process. I'm doing my bit!

Back in the dressing room, the lads are reading sections of some of their fan letters aloud and squawking over some of the declarations of lurve. It's all very boisterous and I think they may be getting a bit bored and unruly.

A costume-department lady arrives to ask what they're wearing for the show. They've decided on white T-shirts but some will wear jeans, black or navy or blue, some cargo trousers, and so on. And the Dork wants to wear his woolly hat, which I think is a mistake.[‡]

I've got their Ten Guitars friendship bands too, and that'll be another matching thing they'll have. It's time to broach a potentially touchy subject[6]. . . I clear my throat and go for it.[§]

---

‡ But, then again, his hair is probably *manky* underneath and not fit to be shown to the public, so maybe it's wise that he's opted for this?

6 I.e. some people wanting to make money off the back of the guys' success.

§ If I don't, my life will be even less worth living than the terror I dwell in now = the wrath of Dixie = worse than this = nuff said.

'As you all know, my friends and I make things to sell at school and we were wondering if we could do these as merchandising?' I hold up the bands. 'If that's OK with you all? It gives fans a chance to show their support . . . and so on . . .'

'Scratchin' a buck,' the Dork says, nodding. 'Very enterprising. Fine by me.'

'Well, Jen isn't getting paid for the fan-club stuff, so I guess the bands are allowable,' Dermot says.

There is general agreement on this point, so I get to text Uggs and Dixie to say: **friendship bands are a go. All will wear them tonite on live TV!**

Looks like we're mini captains of industry again.

I have another thought and text Dixie again: **Gaz v 4 it, may have swayed others?**

I get back: **C? he good! goodenuf anyhow . . .**

Then the composure carpet is pulled from under me. Stevie Lee B strolls over, gets his band and says, 'You better tie this on for me.'

I cannot look him in the eye. If I do, my hands will shake even more than they are already and I'll blush very hard or dribble.

I think I say 'flerb' or something equally lame and nonsensical.

'They're fiddly,' he says, maybe to calm me? 'But good. I love the colours.'

'GERG,' I say, too loudly. Meaning 'good', of course, but sounding like I have lost the ability to speak properly, or in a language that other humans understand.

If he knows that I have a pash for him, I'll DIE! It would be *so* uncool for him to know that a twerpy kid like me is mad about him. I'd be MORTO. I decide immediately and fervently that he can *NEVER* know. And this is a wish that I promise myself I will be true to . . . TILL I DIE!!!!

When I have made a ham-fisted knot, I look up at him and he gives me a wink. EEEK! He *must* know. I scowl at him, without meaning to, and retreat to my writing table. He doesn't seem to notice, which is probably for the best? This is all a minefield and my poor system** is in TATTS right now. Being in lurve is tough and uncomfortable, and I wonder why people do it and even praise it sometimes.

I barely have time to dwell on this thought when the

** I.e. every last, little, painful SHRED of me.

Dork arrives at my side saying, 'You'd best do mine too . . . can't manage it.'

Well, that's the opposite end of the romantic spectrum for me, so I can relax. I even flash Gary some teeth, which may or may not look like a smile. In a way, he's kind of saved me from making a further eejit of myself.[††] I should actually be grateful to him, but that's something he'll never know.

†† Ironic, seeing as he's *such* a numpty . . . but, then again, we all seem to have our moments, if my recent behaviour is anything to go by.

THINK TWICE

I don't understand time.

I know, I know: 'Shock revelation! Hold the front page!' and all that. But I don't understand it.

Like, and par example, time sometimes CRAWLS along – usually when you really need it to pick up some serious pace and get you out of:

a) whatever mess you've got yourself into, or

b) were helped into by others,* or even

c) a mess that will happen (caused by you,

---

* Usually your nearest and dearest, in my thirteen years of experience . . . unless it's Gypsy, and she ain't near or dear to me.

others, or you and others) if time doesn't rev up
and prevent an opportunity occurring for mess-
ing up.

Other times, when you are having a very nice
experience and would dearly like to savour it, it flies, v
v fast and fleetingly. Zoom, there it is, GONE!

Everything gets all sudden and rushed now. The dress
rehearsal is called and everyone is dashing about. I
decide to sit it out, because I want to see the live show
tonight as it's happening on TV, for the nation – I don't
want to spoil it by watching this run-through. I know
what the Guitars are doing, but I want the rest to be
new, even if the 'NEW' is great and therefore worryingly
competitive.

The guys get into their gear, grab a guitar each[†] and
spill out of the room in a flurry of chat and agitation.

I am abandoned in a mountainous pile of Ten Guitars'
debris, including a rather fetching shirt 'n' cardi combo
that (the God) Bolton was wearing earlier and which I
suspect might be a Crimbo pressie, though happily a

---

† That'll be ten guitars, so! Ay, thank you, ay'm here all
day . . . and the next weeks too, if the lads get through.

less embarrassing rig-out than it might have been. Or maybe he's just gorge enough to carry it? Or maybe I am horribly biased and see him through rose-tinted specs and all that. Wotevs: he wears it well, or he *wore* it well, cos right now he's in a white tee and NO ONE wears one of those better than SLB . . . le sigh!

It might be a bit mad to say it, but the room seems to be ringing with the absence of Ten Guitars, like there is an echo of their departure still banging *almost* silently off the walls. I tidy up a few bits and pieces and nibble on a scone that survived the latest bout of teenage scoffage. In fairness, it is a bit bashed at the edges (probably from the tussle of grabbing at the plate) but it's good and still has a few raisins, and that's adding to my five-a-day target, surely.

Then I sit at my table and, although there are some letters still to answer, I find myself wondering what to do next. The life has gone out of the room.

I'm on my own. I'm in charge . . . of me, Jenny Q.

For me, the trouble with down time is that I have far too *much* time to THINK about things. This thinking would be fine if it involved practical, active things, like sorting homework or knitting projects in my head, which, of course, leads to list making and I *love* a good list-making session. But it's when the thinking gets on to big life stuff (emotions and relationships and so on) that the trouble starts. You see, with me, thinking leads to OVERthinking, and then I get myself into knots and can't find my way out and I end up with problems I never had before and they never seem to quite go away as ideas, no matter how hard you try to banish them. And every time they return they have somehow multiplied. They're like the amoebas we learned about in biology that just divide and increase all the time. In other words, thinking is its own problem and that problem leads to more problems.

Complicated and uncomfortable, if you ask me.

So, problems *so far* are . . . (drum roll, anyone?)

a) My dad is only employed part-time now, which means we are bankrupt (I guess) or certainly headed that way. He's not getting any younger,[‡] so that makes it even harder for him to fight for a new job.

b) We have a new baby – not a problem as such,

‡ The guy is in his forties, for goodness sake!

but he needs looking after! He has been brought into the world whether he likes it or not,[6] so he's our responsibility. It all means there are more of us to be fed and clothed and housed, although Harry is on mummy-draught-milk at the moment, so feeding him is not one of the economic problems we have just yet.

c) My mum has gone a bit bonkers, and isn't showing any signs of improvement. This is getting more and more worrying, but I don't know how to help. And in the meantime I feel she is becoming less like my mum every day.

d) My gran IS bonkers – this is a perennial[§] problem and not one that we can do anything about really. It just has to be accepted and sighed over.

e) Everyone I know is broke, including me.

f) My Bestest Galpal, Dixie, is on the hunt for lurve and bound to get herself (and poss/prob

---

6 He does like it, though; you can tell just looking at him.

§ call it perpetual, never-ending, forever - there are many great words that could be used here.

Uggs and me) into a scrape.

g) Gypsy – nuff said . . .

These are not necessarily all as worrisome as each other. Everything is so jumbled in my head right now that I can't think which to tackle first, which is perhaps a problem in itself. Arg!

Then last, but by no means least, on the list is the Supremo Everlasting Problemo . . .

h) I have a pash for a guy who will never return my affections – it is written in the annals of LIFE that he never can = FACT = *true* fact.

Problem h) is where things get outlandish in my head and the overthinking can really get a hold. You see, thinking and overthinking this one, I realize that maybe I love that my lurve for SLB is hopeless.

Say *what*, Jen?

Well, if it weren't, I'd be SO embarrassed.

That is to say, if he showed attention to me and I had to be attentive back, I wouldn't know what to do,

or where to look,

 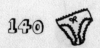

or how to look,

or where to BE,

or even how to *be* the shape of *me*, which I usually am (I'd say) most days.

I need the romance of him not knowing I am alive, romance-wise, otherwise I'd have to be some sort of fabuloso romantic heroine-type for real, instead of just in my head . . . it would be too, too difficult.

It must NEVER be real, unless it is a little bit, a manageable bit. Like, say, him looking wan and thin because he realizes that he lurves me but it is hopeless (how could he EVER be with me?! cos I am way out of his league, even though I am much younger and may grow into a totes nightmare and not the woman of his dreams, which I might be now in this hypothetical situation??), and therefore he must suffer valiantly in silence.

And without (much) bodily contact.

Without, for instance, any spit(tle) having to change company in kisses?**

** Dixie says actual snogging is a wet business and I so do not like the sound of that. Uggs has no real opinion on it and I suspect that, like me, he has never had more than a peck, either on the lips or simply on the cheek.

141

Oh. My. Actual. I am sitting in a dressing room in the biggest gig venue in Dublin, waiting to see my compadres battle it out on TV and I am in the throes of an *imaginary* romance and giving it headspace = that is as mad as people talking about Gypsy as if she knows what they're on about!

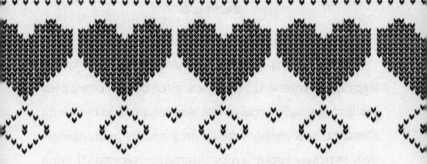

SHOW TIME

When they get back, the lads are lit up like very bright and sparkling fireworks. The noise in the room is up to ninety million decibels of delight, proof that the rehearsal was good for them. They all beam and look pleased. I find myself laughing and clapping and I didn't even watch the thing!

Now to tackle the gluggy/nothing bit between here and show time. Mel is on to it (natch!) and sends in burgers, beans, chips, fish 'n' chips, crisps, chocolate and cola: everything a teen wants/NEEDS to get into 'the zone'. And don't worry: there is hummus and carrots too (which I feast on).*

* This is the totes coolest choice for a cool/chic chick like moi.

There is a lot of spraying out food while chatting because everyone is SO hyped. Weirdly the Dork puts his arm casually around me when I am standing with Dermot, as if simply leaning on a nearby leany-thing — don't know whether to be insulted or worried. I don't want to wreck his buzz, so I leave him be. We live in interesting times right now, let's roll with them!

Make-up ladies come and dab on concealer where it's needed† and powder everyone up to be a matt complexion, not shiny, at least for the beginning of the show.‡

We suddenly become *the* Place to Be. When I look around, I see Delia has joined us. She says she banished her parents to the audience early because they were fussing and making her crazy and even more nervous than she is making herself.

Then a tiny face looks around the door and it's Jess.

Everyone gets introduced to everyone else and I must say the hubbub is LOUD. There is a lot of mutual admiration going on and that's v good and, I suppose, a bit 'phew', because there's no room for daggers'

---

† Teens have zits, though I don't need to tell you that!

‡ All bets are off for later.

 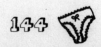

comments here, with the contestants needing all their self-confidence to go out in front of so many people LIVE on TV. Maybe there'll be sniping in a few weeks' time when there's a lot more at stake? And less people to love, of course, with acts going home after each live show. Cripes, I'm getting cynical – Dix says it's realism,[6] but I'm not so sure.

Mel comes back and tells everyone to get set because the show airs in thirty minutes. There is a hush as that sinks in, then an explosion of activity as guitars are tuned and voices warmed up and visits to the loo are made. All of the guys' phones are beeping with GOOD LUCK texts and they talk to their families and loved ones. Then we walk the corridor to the backstage area, a journey that seems v v lengthened, like we're walking through a quicksand of pre-show nerves.

Standing in the wings, I wish all the guys the best of luck and we all swap hugs. Best of all for me is that

6 Reality can be tough, and a bit tougher sometimes than any of us might like it to be. So is realism not a mean first cousin of that? 'Discuss', as our English teacher, Miss Harding, might say.

145

Stevie Lee seems to hang on a little longer than he needs to. And I'm nearly sure he's shaking a little.

'Mad, isn't it?' he says. 'It's like Ireland's very own Gladiator Games. We're being sent out to entertain the masses.'

'Well, yeah, except you're not going to die,' I say.

He laughs a little. 'No, hopefully not even in a showbiz way! WE are the ones about to do the slaying.'

'That's the attitude. Now get out there and *kill*.'

He beams and holds my eye a tad longer than is truly comfortable. Then he says, 'Jen,' and sort of shakes his head and that's confusing – I don't know if it's in a good or bad way. It's *ambiguous*§ and that's unsettling. Time to scuttle sideways and away,** methinks.

I slip into the audience to a small cordoned-off area at the side of the stage reserved for family and friends. I am so nervous for the guys I can hardly swallow or breathe.

§ *Ambiguous* is a grey area, like something just can't or won't make its mind up about what it wants to be. You don't know where you stand with *ambiguous*.

** My star sign is cancer, so the sideways scuttle is a default setting for me.

Show Time

Then the lights in the auditorium dim and a deep voice asks us to switch off our mobile phones. Everyone pretends to but secretly just turns them to vibrate or silent. The familiar *Teen Factor X* theme tune begins to play and the audience starts to scream with anticipation. It is the loudest sound I have ever heard or have ever been part of, and I think I might burst with excitement. The show starts and we all go a bit wild.

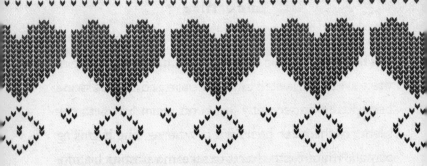

PERFORMING

K.

So . . .

I have NEVER been so totally ENVELOPED in a sound like this! We are all MAD for *Teen Factor X*. This is all flashing lights, music and *us*, SCREAMING our approval for the show and all who appear on it. WE WANT OUR FAVOURITES! I see banners and posters all over the venue – a lot for Ten Guitars.*

Margo, Our Fabliss Presenter, is TRANSFORMED from the early-morning (cantankerous) wreck I saw in

* And these HAVE to be from and by people who don't know the guys, just love them as fans = amazeballs!

the tracksuit.[†] Now she shimmers down the steps of the set positively *sparkling* in a short, royal-blue dress bedecked with sequins. This is no mean feat with the height of the killer heels she is wearing. She is smiling some v white teeth that look like the posting bit of a postbox filled with perfect whiteness. I bet she even smells fantastical! We could not love her more – we scream and wail our appreciation.

We all know how it goes. We scream. They deliver our heroes. We scream again. Lots. First, there'll be an intro on the screens around us – on TV at home it'll just be a 'package' delivered to the domestic screen.[‡] It's v v slick and I am wobbly about the Guitars' piece, though I know they are great. They are at the mercy of the people who want to send the message – it is the show's version of the group that is going to be transmitted. I still think it'll be great.

Margo tells us how marvellous everything in *Teen Factor X* land is and that it's time to welcome our judges. A big door opens at the back of the set and out they

† OK, I shared a pic of that . . . simple back-up for my anecdotes, is all . . .

‡ Mel has been helping me with all the TV lingo.

come, light streaming from behind the three of them. Some fireworks go off down front. We scream v v much and v v loudly.

These people are LEGENDS. We adore them. They are critical, nice, mean, funny and deadly.[6] Danny Faller was the lead singer in a boy band called Bulls and they had a huge hit with 'We Don't Take No Bullshizz'. Now he manages bands. Nicki Richie is a kind of professionally fabliss woman who does a bit of everything – acting, singing, presenting – and she is so good looking it's ridic.[§] Last and by NO means least is Tate Goodwin, impresario, the hardest man to please in showbiz. He looks like he's had some hair added since we last saw him. They wave and go to sit at their huge desk.

We are edging closer to the first act and I know it's the Guitars. They must be bricking it backstage right now! Then Margo announces it's time for the games to begin properly and the screen is full of the lads doing their 'thang'. And then suddenly *I*, too, am on screen –

6 calling something or someone 'deadly' is a great compliment in Ireland.

§ There is no such thing as a bad photo of Nicki R known to humankind, even when she's not wearing make-up.

EEP! And EEK too! Gary is saying, 'This is the lovely Jenny Q, who looks after our correspondence.' The rest of the room cheers – I don't remember that.

Dixie texts: **ur on TV!!**

Uggs: **foxy jen**

I am numb. I don't know how I feel about it or how I looked or anything. A hand touches my elbow and when I look I see it's Delia's mum and she gives me a thumbs up.

I don't have to spend time analysing it all because it's time for the guys to do their number. They have chosen 'The Boys Are Back in Town' by Thin Lizzy. The first chords strike up and a light picks out Dermot, Stevie Lee and the Dork singing. The crowd goes mental. With each line of the song more of the band join in and then they all start to walk to the front of the stage for the chorus. It is magical, no doubt about it. They perform v^{**} well.

I get lots of texts including Dixie: **wow! Gaz lukin v cute 2**

True, he did well and looked OK, I guess, if you like that sort of thing, and (clearly) my Bestie does.

** v to the power of n, which is infinite!!!

151

Dixie: **luv da wristbands = kerching!**

Dix is a businesswoman, can't help herself.

The judges are full of praise – natch! They are not without some quibbles too.

'You're not all great singers, but that almost doesn't matter,' Nicki says. 'The performance is great and exciting to watch.'

The crowd screams delight.

Tate Goodwin gives his verdict: 'You may not all be brilliant musicians, but seeing you all together is some weird kind of genius. It works for me.'

More screaming of approval.

Danny adds, 'You guys are all about spectacle and entertainment and I love that.'

There's screaming at a decibel that may not have been recorded until now. Banners are waved. I actually find it moving and can feel tears well up in my eyes. It's like how I feel when I watch sport on TV, especially people running, for some reason: when they do well, I want to cry with happiness.[††]

And suddenly the lads are off and there is a rare

[††] Bet that's what Mum is doing right now too, if her recent behaviour is anything to go by.

silence, and in that I find my nose tickling v much and I can't control it and then I give a whopper of a sneeze – so much so that it rings out throughout the venue and Margo says, 'Bless you,' from the stage. There is a big laugh. I am SO thankful to be in the darkness of the audience, though the fact that I am so close to the stage must have meant I was caught on the mikes.

Texts are immediate – Dixie: **dat was u!**

And Uggs: **heard u there!**

And Dad: **JEN!**

WHAT?!

I absolutely cannot help myself – how do they know? I have to know how they know! I text and ask.

Dixie: **u do a lil whif b4**

Uggs: **lil sound b4 da sneze**

Dad: **s'how u blow!**

Jeepers, you think you know yourself and THEN . . .

153

LAFFS

We are on to a magician from Waterford now. Sudden, and random or *what*? This is the world of the show, though, and everything is for the delight of the audience, both here in the performance centre and on the TV.

The cheers and noise from the fans never lets up. This audience is ravenous for its favourites.

Jess sings a brillo song about how much fun it would be for her guy to spend the day with her, like feed ducks, fly kites, eat ice cream, get scratched by cats when you try to pet them, blow up balloons and let them go. I can make up new words to old songs and Mum and I sing these new ditties to one another to make us smile. But I could never write a song of my own. At least I don't think so. I love her song and her voice, which is big and strong, even though she is teenchy small. Where does that huge sound come from? She is a belter. The judges are well impressed too.

I text Dixie and Uggs: **vote for jess 2, she v nice + v good**

Suddenly it's time for Delia, which means the show is almost over. It has just sped by and we are all now nearly hoarse with cheering. She comes on looking v miserable, wearing a Christmassy hat, shaped like the Cat in the Hat would wear. When she reaches the front of the stage, she blows a party horn and glumly goes, 'Ho ho ho,' and the audience are laughing and eating out of her hand. She tells the story of Christmas in her house and it's like what happened in every house in the country and it's so, so funny. The horror of people wearing stupid sweaters, and paper crowns from the crackers and trying not to kill one another because of being cooped up together for so long. The pong of mushy Brussels sprouts and turkey curry off everyone and everything. 'You see,' she says, 'it's a fine line between loving someone or something and loathing them.' Then she looks at Danny Faller and says, 'So, you like a

spectacle, Dan? Well, these are spectacles.' She puts her glasses on. 'Like I say, it's such a fine line. Thank you and goodnight.'

Cue MASSIVE cheering. Margo goes over to her and says, 'Delia, not one but two acts from Oakdale. What's in the air out there?'

'Madness, Margo,' Delia tells her. 'And rain, lots and lots of rain.'

Dixie texts: **delia thomas now ofishly a ledgebag!**

It's true, our Delia is a legend.

There is a fabbo recap of our *TFX* night on the huge screens around the arena and it's thrilling to be reminded of all the acts, to see them again,* but also so exhausting to realize all of what has gone before. Then, while there's a TV ad break, we all get voting on our phones and I presume the nation is doing that too!

After the break, Nicki sings her latest single and that's spectac, BUT everyone really just wants more of tonight's teens. They all come back on to the stage to hear the results. Jess and Delia stand with the Guitars

---

* There is a v swoonmostmaking shot of SLB, which is now a candidate for Pic of the Year in my mind.

and that looks natural and righteous to me. Hey, these are my peeps, for gorgonzola-sake.

Margo does the agonizing wait before she announces the acts that have gone through. It's designed to be torture and it IS! In the silences as we wait there's the odd shout of 'we love you' for various contestants.

'In no particular order,' Margo says, and then announces that Jess is through. We scream. Then a dance troupe. We scream. Then Delia. We scream. Then some tap-dancing twins. We scream. Why are the Guitars not through yet? A clarinet player makes it to the next round. We scream. The result might not be in any particular order but I *bet* it's to wind up the tension. And it's doing just that! Then, after a hundred thousand showbiz years, Ten Guitars *are* through and the audience screams and jumps up and down, and so do the guys onstage. I am wrung out, hoarse, feeling hot and clammy but so relieved and happy.

The play-off for the last place is between the magician and the contortionist. The contortionist goes home.

Then Margo tells us all to tune in next time for more teen battles and I can't believe it all has to happen again. I'm wrecked after a day of it. I somehow think I might not be cut out for a showbiz life, whether on the road or simply backstage. I don't think I have the energy for it!

All around me, everyone looks happy. One show down, and we are into the semi-final!

POST-SHOW

Everyone seems to gather in the Guitars' room for the post-show celebration. Jess and Delia are getting a lot of attention from the guys and I must admit I feel a *lil* twinge of something that I presume is jealousy. I understand it, though. All those who performed tonight looked so attractive onstage that it's natural they want to praise one another now for jobs v v well done. Hell, even Gary O'Brien looked OK up there.

Ooops, be careful what you wish for, Jennifer Quinn: here he comes now to talk to you.

'Some night, eh?'

'Totes. I can hardly speak for the screaming.'

'Yeah, the sound of it was awesome.'

I give a few sneezes out of nowhere. I need a tissue fast before I become a liquidy snottynose. Mel appears at my shoulder brandishing one.

'You may have fallen prey to the curse of the studio lurgy,' she says. 'Being cooped up here all day means you're mostly breathing in recycled air and every passing germ has a chance to get at you.'

Delia says, 'I've always thought Santa Claus must get that too, when he's in the stores meeting kids – every germ in town gets to breathe into his beardy face so he must be riddled with disease all the time, colds and flu, you know? As well as smelling every foul, childish breath imaginable.'

'Kids stink,' I agree, following it up with a massive, whooshy double-sneeze.

The Dork clearly doesn't want to catch anything, so he moves off to do some backslapping and high-fiving.

'That guy is so busting a move on you,' Mel says. 'Has been all day.'

'*WHAT?!*' I squeak in the tiny voice I have left.

'Don't tell me you haven't noticed. He can't stop grinning when you're around and he's been staring at you, like, *lots*, and then trying to chat any time he got a chance. It's kinda cute.'

NO, IT IS NOT CUTE! This is bad news, v bad news *indeed*.

Number a) he is Gary the DORK O'Brien, and
Number b) I only have eyes for Stevie Lee Bolton,
      and, most pertinent of all,
Number c) my Bestie Galpal Dix has her sights set
      on him, so he is a no-go area (thank goodness).

It'll pass, I tell myself, this is all just heat-of-the-moment stuff because we have had the oddest day in the history of our lives so far and everything is a bit wonky as a result. It will pass. It *has* to pass. Even though I feel feverish, I now get the shakes at how much I need this situation to pass, dissolve, disappear. It will be gone by tomorrow, I reason, once we are all home and back to the normal we are used to. There, problemo solved, shelved, forgotten.

Or maybe not. The Gazmeister is back and puts an arm around my shoulder saying, 'You are our lucky charm, Jen.'

I let rip a mega-sneeze that sprays a bit out into the air in front of us and he backs off again for fear of

161

infection. A cold might be a handy thing for warding off an unwanted Guitar.

Outside the venue the band gets MOBBED by fans wanting photos, autographs, hugs. It's NUTS. I have a sneaking suspicion that the Slinkies would not like to see our Oakdale boys being adored and grabbed like this. I'm not sure I love it myself. And it's not just girls – there are lots of lads too, cheering for their new heroes. Jess and Delia get huge cheers when they emerge, but it's easier to get them past the madness into their cars to be sent home. We're trying to load ten teenage boys on to a bus. As Gran would say, 'It's like herding cats.'

Finally, the rain starts up again and that concentrates everyone on keeping dry, so we board the bus once again and head for Oakdale. It was dark when we set out this morning and it's dark as we go home. We never saw daylight, so maybe today didn't really happen? And maybe we are a *tad* vampire, after all, active only in the dark hours? I'm probably hallucinating now with tiredness, excitement and the head cold that is trying to stuff up my nose. Showbiz, anyone? I honk into my hankie. Oh, the glamour of it.

RUNNY SUNDAY

Every bit of my body aches when I wake up the next morning. My nose* is bunged up and I seem to have breathed through my mouth all night and therefore it is dry as the Sahara and my throat has a thorny thorn bush in it. I may also have been snoring. Lovely, NOT!

I lurch downstairs and into the kitchen. Mum takes in the shell of her only daughter and says, 'Poor Jen!' so I must look as awful as I feel.

'What if I give this to Harry?' I wail. I'm going to have to forgo my hugs for a while till I am less, well, catching, and already that is unbearable.

* Now pronounced 'by doze' by my good self.

Gran arrives and makes an X with her arms to ward off my germs.

'Not funny,' I squawk, in a voice that's much lower and quieter than usual.

'But it means you have an X factor yourself now,' she tells me, delighted with her own wit.

'Hex factor, more like,' I say.

A hot, lemony drink is put in front of me and I sit trying to inhale it, while it's cooling to drinking temperature, to clear 'by doze'. It works well enough to get me streaming again. As Delia Thomas might say of my nose, 'This one will run and run.' There's probably a late Christmas gag about me being Rudolph in there too, but my head is mush and not thinking straight.

When we're all gathered, Dermot and I report on the recording, how it was to experience it live. It's all taped for us to watch later.

'Harry loved it,' Mum says. 'He sat staring at the screen while you were on.'

Dermot nods. 'The kid's got taste.'

'We were so proud of you,' Mum tells him. 'Of you both. You looked so well and the performance was great.' Her eyes are filling up but she shakes the tears away. Thanks be to flip for that. There's enough liquid coming out of my face to do this whole family. And if Mum starts crying again, I will be crushed.

It's like she can read my mind. 'I laughed out loud at Delia's routine,' she says. 'So I haven't forgotten how to do that.'

It doesn't ease my worry that she has changed for ever and maybe not for the better. I want my old mum back: the chatty, smiley one. Suddenly, everything feels a bit much and I decide this will be a pyjama day because I feel so YUCK. I will hold court in my room, with the Gang, and start on my bath rug. I may even get brought treats because everyone feels sorry for me.[†]

Dixie texts: **r u infectious?**

Me: **maybe?**

Dixie: **well enuf to work?**

Me: **EH?**

Dixie: **crochet plaits! No root, no fruit**

Jeepers, can a gal not take to her bed in peace with a rotten cold any more?

Me: **hands stil workin**

Dixie: **phew/gud**

[†] Including me!

165

Ripping up my duvet cover is sad. It has covered me for years, kept me warm in winter and cool in summer. I feel an emotional tie to it and I hope it doesn't mind the change. I convince myself it's almost karmic that it is to live on in another form and therefore a v good thing for the world.

Ennyhoo, I lay it on my desk and cut the beginnings of the strands, two centimetres apart. Then I rip the cover using my hands. It's a tip I found on the internet and it makes for a much straighter line than using scissors to cut the whole way. The ripping sound is v impressive and vigorous. I like doing things like this that don't require too much brain work because they allow me to daydream if I want, or just to zone out, like now, because my head is mankified with this lurgy.

Uggs and Dix are well impressed when they see my work. I had told them about my foxmost plan for the bath mat, but seeing it begin to happen before their eyes gets it a further thumbs up. Thumbs down is that Gypsy has decided to help me by lying on the pile of shreds that I am trying to knot together into a ball of cotton yarn. At least I can't smell her doggy breath because I am bunged up again.

Runny Sunday

Dixie claps her hands. 'Knitting in hand, please, it's time to (k)natter.' You can't have one without the other, you see. She is going to tackle the friendship bracelets. Uggs is making a start on compiling yarns for the Valentine gifts.

'I'm a romantic at heart,' he tells us. 'If that sniplet of info goes further than this room, you die.'

'I'm glad you brought up l'amour,' says Dixie. 'Because I have been getting some attention. Last night I had a lovely online "chat" on Facebook with a new friend.'

We sort of stop and stare, which Dixie takes as positive encouragement.

'His name is Kev and we really hit it off.'

'What do we know about this Kev?' Uggs asks.

'Not much, really, except that he's v v nice.'

'How did you meet him on there?'

'He messaged me, saying he couldn't help but notice me because he's single too, after a bit of a shocker with a girlfriend, so maybe we should hook up.'

'What do you mean, "hook up"?' I ask.

'Well, we'll keep in touch online and if there's a chance for us to meet, we will.'

'Have you even seen a picture of this guy?' Uggs wants to know.

'Not yet. He's going to send me some.'

'Might be dodge, Dix.'

'Nah. I have a good feeling about him.'

Hmmm, I don't have any such good feeling and I can see from Uggs that he doesn't either. Sometimes Dixie is so gung-ho in her 'can do' attitude that she doesn't follow sensible rules. This guy is a stranger and until we know more about him there is NO WAY we'll let her meet him.

FEELIN' HOT HOT HOT!

I give up on trying to do my bath mat because Gypsy is in love with my newly invented yarn. I wonder if she knows it was a duvet cover and therefore it lived on my bed and therefore it is something she used to lie on at every opportunity.*

We make lots of 'product' (as Dixie insists we call the Ten Guitar bracelets) while she makes up what

---

* Even if I didn't love her doing that,† which probably spurred her on to new levels of determination to lay claim to my bed. †I still don't love her being on my bed, but she ignores me and does her own thing regardless.

she's calling a 'prototype' of the love hearts for Vally's Day.

I have to run through all the details of my day on *Teen Factor X*, which is a little bit of a minefield in places because I can't mention Mel's theory that Gary O'Brien was paying me special attention. In fact, I don't want to believe it anyhow, so perhaps it's a blessing (in disguise) that Dixie's interest in him means the whole thing is off limits.

'By doze' is blocked again and I cannot taste my Kit Kat. I can tell it's sweet and lovely, though, don't know how. Actually, that's *one* good thing about Gypsy:[†] she's not allowed chocolate for humans as it is v bad for dogs. This cheers me, always, and not even in a v mean way. It's probably a relief that there is one legitimate area where I can say 'no' to her and know it's for her own good![‡]

When the Gang has finished our Knit 'n' Knatter, I wave them off and become a knotter again to finish preparing my bath-mat material. I'm still achy and I really don't feel v good, so I bag an armchair in front of

[†] Probably the only good thing.

[‡] Snigger . . .

the fire downstairs and start to cast on my stitches. It doesn't last long because I feel waves of tiredness and my eyes drooping and the next thing I know Dad is shaking me awake.

'Hey there, sleepy head. Wakey-wakey. You've been out for an hour and a half.'

My head is sore now and I am really thirsty and feeling far too hot. In normal circs when I feel seedy and horrid I like a cuddle from Mum, but I am way too boiled for that. Anyhow, she's sitting gazing at the TV in a way that tells me she's not paying any attention to what's on.

'Earth to Mum,' I say, and she doesn't notice that either.

'Stop teasing your mother,' Gran says to me in a quiet voice.

I feel so rotten with my cold I nearly ask, 'Why are you not in your own gaff?' but it doesn't seem worth the effort because it will SO end in grief and it *is* also a bit nasty.[6]

For an awful moment I suspect Gran is here because she's cooking for the family tonight, then I realize that

6 Like this vile head cold!

171

even if she is I am safe because I can't taste anything. I also don't feel like eating, but Gran has declared that it is best to 'feed a cold and starve a fever', so I'll be forced to dine whether I like it or not (though, hopefully, none of it will matter because my taste buds are wonkified). Janey Mac, how can a routine Sunday evening be so complicated?

In the end, we have beans on toast and even Gran can't muck that up. Dermot has surfaced to be fed. Most of the day he's been holed up in his room, but that's not unusual for him. His phone beeps constantly with texts about the show and every so often I hear him talking on it too.

Some of the calls are about what number to do for the semi-final. It's head-wrecking to know it all has to be repeated so soon. I hear him talking to Sam Slinkie too and it doesn't sound like they're having a big love-in, which is v intriguing to say the least! I hear him say, 'I think that's a bit unreasonable,' and, 'Well, whatever, your choice.' Oooh!

Then I am piled high with cough and cold medicine and sent to bed. It's lovely to crawl under my duvet and surrender to sleep. The last thing I remember is Stevie Lee telling me I smelled lovely on the early-morning bus and I am sure I fall asleep with a smile on my red-nosed face.

S'CRUEL

I like school, in general, but it rhymes with 'cruel' and sometimes that ain't no co-inki-dink. This Monday morning is not beginning itself well for me. I have a pounding headache and v little voice. My throat is raw and my limbs feel leaden. BUT I am determined to go to school because it is totes *unthinkable* to miss the first day back after the show and all the action and chat that will bring along with it. Besides, I have a postbox to attend to and money to make. I may feel cruddy, but as the song says, L.I.F.E.G.O.E.S.O.N.

The Assembly hall is *BUZZING* with talk of the show. The Guitars are getting slapped on the back and Delia is congratulated by anyone who can get near her through her crowd of admirers. She looks a bit bemused by it all. She is one person when she's performing or on TV and another in 'real life'. I wonder if it'll get to her eventually that everyone expects her to be funny all the time, and that they think they must tell her all their bad jokes too!

The principal just can't help himself as he addresses Assembly. He tells us, 'I know you were all very proud of your schoolmates, but remember you are here to be educated. And to our wonderful contestants, do remember that too. You boys are back in town and I wouldn't like you or Delia making spectacles of yourselves.' He gives a little laugh as if at his own devilish cleverness, but mostly to show that he has made a joke in case we missed it. OUCH!

He's clearly proud as punch to reveal that he:

a) is watching the show and

b) has a sense of humour and

c) is 'hip' with us kids.

We all stand with our mouths hanging open.

'Oh. My. GROAN,' Dixie groans. 'He really did that, didn't he? He really just said that, he *went* there.'

'Adults should stay away from making jokes,' I say. 'They have a weird sense of humour.'

'Agreed. Embarrassing,' is Uggs's verdict.

When will it happen to us, I wonder, as we grow up? It's like, when does a lamb stop bouncing and jumping around and suddenly become a sheep that just eats grass and not much more?

My dad loves words and can't resist puns as a result. He often makes a groanworthy quip and says, 'Do you see? Do you see what I did there?' just to rub it in.*

We always go, 'Yes, Dad, we see,' sighing sadly at his effort.

'Blinded by it,' Dermot once told him.

Delia sidles over and says, 'I feel I should apologize for causing that groanworthy display from the Head.'

'You're only partly responsible,' I tell her. 'There are ten other people in the mix with you.'

'Musicians,' Uggs says, nodding at the splendid villainy of that. 'Rebels and troublemakers always, since the dawn of time.'

Delia brightens. 'Great, so. Rabble-rousing is a fine way to start the week.'

* or simply *emphasize* it, as he thinks.

176

S'cruel

We all laugh at that because we all feel a bit involved and naughty. It feels good. Unlike my general head area, which is fuzzy and throbbing.

Dixie has made a poster, which she pins to the main school noticeboard.

OFFICIAL TEN GUITARS WRISTBANDS
NOW AVAILABLE
SHOW YOUR SUPPORT!
Handcrafted and only 50c each
Contact Dixie Purvis, Eugene Nightingale or Jenny Q

And, we're off!

'First eight gone already,' she tells us as the bell for class rings and we make our way to double Maths. My face hurts to think of the brainwork I may have to do over the next hour with a head full of, well, snot. Still, we're 'quids up' and that's a warm and happy place, a case of figures adding up, I think, and I groan. Here I am tying everything up, making it relevant to my Maths class, for fruitsake – I must have caught that from the principal and his cringe-making *TFX* speech. My head hurts a little more now that *I* have 'gone there'. Eek!

SO DAMN UNPRETTY

It's lunchtime before I investigate the fan mail in the postbox. And I suppose I should have expected that not everyone would be pleased with the band's success. There is hate mail. The 'you think you're great but you are NOT' stuff and worse. Not much, but enough for me to look around and wonder who in the school is so jealous or so full of bile that they have to write this hateful stuff.* I decide never to show it to the lads.

What I don't understand is why anyone would want to put this sort of stuff into words. Then again, maybe

---

* Ten Guitars are now an obvious target because they're so visible and they're going to get it in the neck from the malcontents and oddballs.

their life is so awful they want to lash out at someone who seems to be doing well? It's a bit of a waste of time (or at least it will be if I hide this stuff), but maybe it makes them feel better to have vented their frustration or whatever. Ennyhoo, it is not nice reading. And of course it's anonymous, so that's a bit cowardly too, as if they can't let themselves be named (and shamed?) and can't even take responsibility for their words.

Delia's box has a lot of 'You're great' and so on[†] and then one that just states, 'You're not funny, you're adopted.' Well, OK, this is getting on my (quite wheezy) chest at this stage. I am fed up of negativity. And the idea that someone might not be funny simply because they're adopted is laughable and impossible, *and* Delia *IS* funny, v v funny! I am going to watch the boxes and find out who these teens with v v bad attitudes are and give them a piece of my mind.[‡]

Dixie appears at my side. 'Business is booming and we're going to have to buy more yarn and make more bracelets toot sweet.'

† She is!

‡ or something . . . I can't decide or think straight while the germs are still gumming up my brain.

Uggs confirms that we are running out of stock. 'Product is low,' he tells me, and winks as he uses Dixie's terms. She doesn't see him, which is lucky for Uggs, because Dixie can be fierce if she thinks she's being teased unfairly.[6]

'Supply and demand,' she says. 'We should tell Poor Mr Mulhall we understand that now.'

Poor Mr Mulhall teaches Economics and everyone has spent so long calling him Poor Mr Mulhall that it has stuck and that's his full name now. For the record, I think he's fairly well off, it's just his unfortunately miserable look and tinny voice that got him his title. When you get a nickname in Oakdale High you keep it.[§]

We get some lunch in the canteen and review the day so far.

'How is this stew?' I ask Uggs, because I can't taste it.

'Quite edible,' he tells me.

'Good enough. I'll tell myself I'm enjoying it, so.'

'My Facebook romance is moving on,' Dixie says.

---

[6] *All* teasing of Dix is unfair in her opinion!

[§] Which is why I do NOT want anyone taking up mouthy Mike Hussy's habit of calling me 'Ginger'.

'Oh?' I try to sound v casual.

'Kev wants me to send more photos.'

'There are already lots of photos of you up there,' Uggs points out.

'Yes, but they're for everyone to see. These would be just between us, special.'

'Has he sent you a pic of him?' I ask.

'He says he will today, after school.'

I *so* don't like the sound of this Kev and I think this photo business is all a bit sneaky . . . and suspect . . .

'We'll have a look at him then,' Uggs says, quite firmly. 'And you shouldn't send him anything until he does.'

'Motion carried,' I say, even though strictly speaking we weren't having a Gang powwow.

Gary O'Brien rocks up and sits at the table with us – well, beside me, to be more exact. Dixie quickly scans the canteen to see if Jason the Tongue Fielding is around and available to notice. He is nowhere to be seen so we are spared my Bestie flinging herself across the table at one of the newest Rock Gods in town. She doesn't even need to talk loudly to gain an audience for this event, because it is a non-event. All of which is a relief.

'How goes it?' GOB wants to know.

We murmur that things are fine.

'Poor old Jen caught the show sneeze, didn't you?' he says.

'Yup.' Sounds like I've said 'YUB', though.

'She was great looking after us on Saturday,' he continues and then (ARGH) he only goes and puts his arm around my shoulder and gives me a squeeze. I am boiled with embarrassment as well as my high temperature from the *TFX* fever = not good.

Dixie's right eyebrow is raised and I know her mind is doing all sorts of somersaults as she works out what she's seeing here. Uggs is trying not to laugh.

'Right, best keep on keepin' on,' he says and lets go of me.** 'Laters.' He strolls over to another table.

'Interesting,' Dixie says, and waits for me to explain myself.

I shrug. 'He's one of the group, they're all glad I'm doing the fan mail.'

The eyebrow is still arched.

** ARGH that he has to let go in the first place, but PHEW too that he does, and that the clutching of the Jenny Q has been brief.

So Damn Unpretty

'Oh, come ON, Dixie! The Dork? Me? I think not.'

'True enough,' she says and I can breathe again.[††]

As we make our way back to class Uggs sidles up and whispers, 'That guy *likes* you.' I thump him on the arm and threaten (no, *promise*) to kill him if he ever says, or even thinks, such a thing again.

I may have become a hypersensitard about this situation, but it's good to be on my guard lest[‡‡] it escalate.

---

†† Through my mouth, by doze is stuffed up still.

‡‡ 'Lest' is a wonderful word. A classy substitute for 'in case' and somehow old fashioned *yet* hip, no?

SHADOWY

The pic of Kev on Facebook is mostly the back of a guy's head moving and maybe laughing. In other words, you can't tell what he looks like, really. His biog info says he goes to school in Wicklow, so it's not like it's going to be easy to hook up with him, because that's miles away, in another county, and southside. Oakdale is northside and within the Dublin city limits. His DOB makes him fifteen and it pleases Dix that he's 'an older man'.

'Was that not what I was looking for?' she says, as if this is the best thing ever and proof that this is the guy for her.

Personally I am beginning to suspect she's secretly reading romantic books or watching smushy movies and living her own life accordingly. I know I do, and it kind of scrambles my head and makes me all gooey.

'Is he online now?' Uggs asks.

'Should be. He usually is.'

'Let's chat with him, so,' I say.

Dixie types in some chat and sure enough this Kev is available.

HIM: Was just thinking about you!

DIX: Ditto

HIM: Great minds and all that. Was also thinking that if you give me your mobile number I can send you pics and vice versa. Much better than doin' it on here where everyone can nosey through them.

'See?' she says. 'He's really into me.'

'I think it's creepy,' I say. 'And he should start by sending proper pics to you here online before any of this exchanging-phone-numbers business.'

'Jen is right,' Uggs says. 'We don't know who this guy is. And this is all the stuff we've been warned about.'

Dixie scrunches up her face in a NOT happy expression and sighs.

'OK,' she eventually says. 'You two are getting so SENSIBLE.'

She does not mean this as a compliment.

'Not everyone out there is a villain,' she says, defensively. 'I suppose I'll just have to concentrate on my lonely-hearts replies.'

'WHAT?!' Both Uggs and I are v loud in our shock. She still has lots of wriggle room for getting into a scrape, whole wide corridors of opportunity for disazzo.

'Did you not think I'd get some?' she asks, in an uppity, attitudey way.

This whole scenario really is going from bad to badder.*

'Thought you'd be thrilled!' There's deffo a hint of mockery creeping into her tone now. 'At least it's going to be someone from one of the local schools, so you can keep an eye on proceedings, if that's what you're both so worried about.'

Looks like we're involved up to our armpits and beyond.

---

* And it is not in any way badass, which is hip and cool.

'There's a chap who wants to meet for coffee in the Barnacle Café. We'll start with him.'

As I predicted, though I neglected to say it aloud to my Gang, we are *all* going on a date with whoever answers Dixie's ads. Eek McEek of Eeksville!

As Uggs and I walk home I ask, 'Should we just shop her to her family and let them deal with it?'

'It might be too drastic a solution,' he says. 'She would also never, and I mean NEVER, forgive us.'

He's right, of course.

'If she is v impossible, and nothing else works, can we agree that we will beat sense into her?'

'Although I am against physical violence, unless it's on a rugby pitch, yes, yes, we will do that.'

'For her own good.'

'Totes.'

Of course, we would never raise a finger to anyone or any creature,[†] so this is all macho talk to keep ourselves calm. We are both worried sick about Dixie – who seems to be going more bonkers than she has

---

† Although I do try shoving Gypsy off my things, but it rarely works.

187

ever been before.[‡] And I *am* actually sick too! Double trouble for Jenneefuh . . .

And the irony is, of course, that we are trying to knit love hearts for Vally's Day. SHEESH!

Yet again, I am happy to *imagine* a romance that can never be with Stevie Lee Bolton – it's by far the safest sort of relationship to have with anyone.

‡ And that's saying something. FACT.

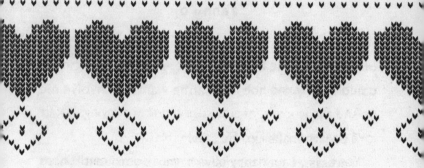

A HELPING HAND

I am barely in the door when Dad appears and goes, 'Jen, excellent. I need your brains.'

This usually means he'll run the spec for an advertisement by me, I will come up with some fabtastico idea for the ad, and he'll steal it and pass it off as his. I don't mean this to sound sour — it's just a fact in the Quinn household. I guess it's because we both love words and painting pictures with them. If Dad ever concedes, even slightly, to my 'theft theory', he says he is merely 'appropriating'* an idea that I will never use and employing it for the good

* This is acquiring rather than robbing, apparently, and therefore not any class of crime (according to Dad).

of all. Now that he's part-time, though, I imagine it could be any old hoo-ha that he wants to involve me in.

'Teenage make-up,' he says.

'Yeessss,' I say carefully. 'I can try to explain us teenagers to you, but for generations grown-ups and teens have been at odds. It's a natural law.'

'No,' he says.

'Yes, I'm afraid so,' I say.

'No,' he reiterates. 'Teen make-up, as in cosmetics.'

'Oh, right. Er, do you want to borrow some?'

'In a way.'

OK, official weirdoid territory now.

'Dad, I'm not sure anything I have will suit you.'

'Funny, Jen.'

Actually, I wasn't trying to be smart, just factual!

'I want to invent a line of make-up aimed at teens. Or invent names for the products. It's a pitch for a new line that's going into production.'

'So you're not going dressed as a schoolgirl to some saddo party?'

'No.'

'Good.'

'It's for a new agency and, if they like my ideas, it might mean I'll get extra work or maybe even a new full-time job.'

This *is* big news.

Just then, Stevie Lee emerges from our front room. I am not sure if it is one of life's nice surprises. I suspect I look wretched and I know my nose is now both dripping *and* red from having walked home in a cold wind. I won't even begin to consider what state my hair is in, but I'd say it is a big and unruly hedge after being buffeted by nature all the way from school via Dixie's.

I give a bit of a wave and flee upstairs to my room. A glance in the mirror shows a scarecrow creature with a red nose AND red eyes = unwelcome development = EEP! I change out of the maroon Oakdale uniform, as it does no one any favours and presently seems to be making me look even paler in general while picking up and accentuating my new red face-highlights. Then I tidy up that face, as much as possible,[†] spray on some dewberry[‡] and I am ready to be seen and smelled again, though it is a *just in case* measure, as I'd prefer to know

† Not much can be done, it's a mess!

‡ A nice smell, according to SLB on Saturday.

191

SLB is in the house and vice versa and just leave it at that. I'm all out of human interaction right now and could do with being left alone.

I race through my homework because Dad has booked me to brainstorm ideas after dinner. By 'brainstorm' we know he means the picking of Jen's brain for her ideas, as previously mentioned and discussed. I don't mind, really, because I think this will be fun, and if it might help Dad's job situ, then I deffo want to help out. We all have to row in for the common Quinn good. Then I spray on some more scent, because I can't smell anything and it may have worn off, and I waft down to the kitchen, ready to see and be seen.

For all my deviousness, I am undone[6] because the mini Guitars' meeting in the TV room has disbanded and the lads are gone home. *Le sigh.* Sometimes a gal can be too clever and aloof for her own good. Still, one less chance to snot 'n' snuffle in front of the god that is Stevie Lee, so mayhap[§] 'tis for the best.

Sausages and mash for dins (NOM!) and then to work.

---

6 As they say in the olden plays – it's got a ring to it that I like.

§ Another ancient wordette that's groovy to my ears.

'What have we got here?' I've been watching a lot of TV and I know how to be tough and direct when opening a business convo.

'A fun range aimed at young teens.'

'Welcome to my world,' I say.

'And mine,' Dad says. 'For a while, anyhow, if they like the ideas.'

'Do you want to go the Young and Sassy route?'

'Sass! That's what we could call the whole thing!'

'OK.' Jeeps, I didn't realize I'd be on a roll quite so soon. Internal high-five to me, from me!

The next hour is real fun and we LOL. 'SASS: for Teens with Tude' is born. Dad fires a product at me and I think of sassy ways to describe it. For example, we have a lip gloss (that no one yet knows may be inspired by the Dork) called:

GOB! Lippy with attitude.

Then for the blusher:**

CHEEKY! It's made to make you blush.

An eye shadow called: PEEPERS! See the world through new eyes.

EYE EYE! (mascara) *Lash* it on for a positive look at life.

** or 'rouge' if you, like me, prefer le français.

TALONTED! (nail varnish) Nail what *you* want.

We're still stuck on a name for the concealer, an *essential* item for a teen, though we know the tag line for it is 'Spot the disguise'.

We have fun with the pun so Dad is happy with that, and I love an excuse to play with words, and we've come up with some cracking ideas = all in all, a win/win sitch.

But I ain't done yet. Hell, no. I am on a ROLL.

'What you really need is to back up these ideas with some hard data that proves how popular SASS would be with teens,'[††] I say. 'Maybe you could canvass[‡‡] the *Teen Factor X* audience? You know, hand out a survey to the queue waiting to get in?'

'Jen, that is a great idea. But I doubt the company would allow it,' Dad says. 'They might want money, or an involvement of some sort, for using their show?'

'Leave it with me, Dad — I have friends in high places.'[◊◊]

[††] Oh yes. I watch *Dragons' Den* and I have the phrases!

[‡‡] Another super business-like phrase, thank you very much.

[◊◊] Surely Mel would help me?!

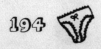
194

Working my brain has taken my mind off the pain of having a cold. My head is aching again now and I am learning to hate the rhythm of it. It's good to be laughing, though, and I only wish Mum was here to join in. She drifted through once to make tea but, barring a wan smile, she hardly acknowledged us. It is making me as sad as she looks. I give Dad a quizzy look, and I think now is the moment I will raise my worries about her. But he says, 'Leave it, Jen, she's not herself.' Hmm, it is not a comfort to hear this.

Gran makes me a hot lemon drink and gives me some aspirin for my pounding head.

'Did ye do good?' she asks about our brainstorm.

'Knocked it out of the park, Gran,' I assure her.

Then Uggs arrives, with you-know-who at his heels barking up a storm. Gran is delighted.

'Did you come to see your granny?' she asks . . . the DOG.

Gypsy yips and jumps and pirouettes.

'You did, you did come to see your granny!'

'She did indeed, Mrs Q.'

Oh, here's a Quinn Quirk I haven't mentioned. My gran is Mrs Q, but she's not a Quinn in that sense. The

Quinn name in our family comes from my dad's side, BUT Mum didn't need to change her initials because her maiden name was Quentin. Hence my gran, her mum, is Connie Quentin, or Connie Q, or Mrs Q.

'Gran, you're acting like a crazy person. You are not her granny!'

'True, Mrs Q, she's not actually a Quinn,' Uggs says.

'NO!' I exclaim, exasperated. 'She's a *dog*.'

'True, Jenny Q,' Uggs agrees. 'She's a dog, Mrs Q. She's problee the gran of *you*. Woohoo!§§ Dog years and all that.'

'Eh, none of the above,' I say. 'Different species, anyone?'

I am ignored.

'Brought you a gift, Jen,' Uggs says, and produces a bath bomb. 'Thought this might help unplugging your sinuses.'

He has made me a special medicinal bomb!

§§ It's like he's practising rhymes for one of our poetry jams and, although he's being v annoying, I have to admit I feel a grudging admiration.

'It's got eucalyptus and stuff in there to help with, like, breathing.'

'Breathing is good,' Dad says with a grin. 'Makes all the difference, really.'

'Well, aren't you the sweetest boy,' Gran remarks. 'And aren't you the lucky girl, Miss Jennifer.'

Gran is stirring it up and both Uggs and I are *squirming*. I have known Uggs for ever and he's like a bro to me! OK, once upon a long-time-ago, according to legend, he said he wanted to marry me, but he was a weeny toddler then, so I don't know why the adults can't let it go, no matter how sweet it was: ancient history = build a bridge and get over it.

There is no doubt, though, that this is a lovely and thoughtful gift. And when people do such lovely things for one another, it is a tiny teeny proof that they love them, BUT this is between friends, Besties, nothing more.

'Ignore them, Uggs,' I say. 'They're strange people.'

When the strange adults are preoccupied elsewhere, Uggs delivers a bomb of another sort – a bomb*shell*.

'In other news, there is no Kev going to the school he says he's going to.'

'Are you sure?'

'Yeah. I got my older bruv, Mal, to check. Made him pretend to be a teacher from Oakdale, told him it'd be good practice for when he actually is a teacher.'

I snort. 'Which one did you make him be?'

'I was tempted by Miss Harding, but Mal's voice is *slightly* lower than hers, so I went for Mr Hannigan, Careers Guidance Counsellor extraordinaire.'***

'Nice. J'approve.'

'It was irresistible, really, and he's an easy one to copy with the twangy voice. I was just terrified that Mal might get someone who actually knows Hannigan – the teaching world is a small one, after all.'

'This leaves us with an almighty problem,' I say.

'Yeah. Who is this Kev guy and what is he up to?'

*** Hannigan is *so* not 'extraordinaire' and anyone who takes his advice deserves all they get for being utter bimbos - harsh but true.

AND BREATHE!

The bomb is Da Bomb! After it has fizzed up a storm, and the bathroom is all lovely and steamy, I lie back in the warm water and breathe it all in. It does clear my pipes, so Uggs is a genius, as well as a sweetie. The warmth of the water is so soothing and breathing in the aroma and vapours is a delight.

It's a good time to take stock of what needs to be done, now that my brain is being freed up from the gack that has been clogging it. I decide to add some knitting to my project list. I will make a patchwork quilt for Harry. It will be simple, really, a collection of various kinds of knitted squares sewn together and looking v v pretty. That's about as far as I get when Mum comes through the door.

EEK! I thought I had locked it, though maybe I just put up the sign that says STAY OUT that we use as a further precautionary measure here at Quinn Central. Dermot even has a plastic yellow cone with a skull and cross-bones on it that declares this a toxic area. That can be deployed as a warning to all others that they should leave ten minutes or so before entering.*

Mum doesn't even see me. OK, the place is steamed up, but would she not at least wonder why? She really is on her own channel right now. It's a major worry.†

She's now sitting on the loo. *Mega* EEP! I am naked in the bath‡ and my mother is on the loo. Spot what's wrong with this picture, much, anyone???

'MUM!' I yelp.

She looks over and smiles. 'Ah, Jen, there you are.'

---

* No need to go into why that might be here, I feel, no need to *elaborate*.

† I feel frustrated that I can't address the problem full on because Dad said to go easy on it all.

‡ And not a bubble bath, with frothiness that might cover my bits!

And Breathe!

Then the penny drops as she notices where we both are. 'Oh, right, I see. Sorry about that. I was away somewhere else.'

'I noticed,' I tell her.

Neither of us feels like striking up a chat,[6] although it is nice to be with Mum and to have her attention, however briefly.

'I'll leave you to it,' she says, and goes.

I can't risk any further invasions, so I have to curtail bath time. I do feel better, though, and I take lovely deep breaths through my nose to savour the clearness of nostril that Doctor Eugene Nightingale has provided. I quickly dry off, get into some fluffy jimjams and climb into bed. I'm propped up against all my pillows reading when Gran pokes in.

'That young fella has a real notion of you,' she says.

I roll my eyes at the idea. 'He's me Best Blokepal, Gran.'

'I brought you this.' She produces a vapour rub for my chest. 'My uncle Marty was a farmer in County Meath, one of the old-style codgers who didn't understand medicine for the animals, or humans either.

6 Given our strange situation . . .

201

He thought if one tablet was good, two was better. And I don't think he ever read the instructions for anything in his life.'

I'm wondering where this is going and if it will be the sort of meandering story Gran is fond of and good at. In other words, this could be a long night.

'Anyhow, I was on holidays there once and I had an awful cough. In the middle of the night he came into the room, grabbed a jar of this stuff and gave me two handfuls of it to *swallow*. I can still taste it!'

See? Is it any wonder this family has evolved into a bunch of lunatics? It's coming down through our genes.

This also goes some way to explaining why Gran thinks odd combos of food are edible.

'Cured the cough, mind you.'

'I won't eat it,' I tell her, with a solemn expression.

'Promise,' she says, equally solemnly.

Then we both laugh. It's nice: what they call a feel-good moment.

It's also clearly visiting time at the zoo, with my room as the fave exhibit, because next up is Dad.

'Just wanted to say thanks for all your help earlier, Jen. Appreciate it. I really enjoyed it too.'

And Breathe!

'Ditto. Fingers crossed they like the ideas, and we can get some info to back them up from *Teen Factor X*.'

He sniffs the air. 'You smell like a little cough drop.'

'I'll take that as a compliment,' I say.

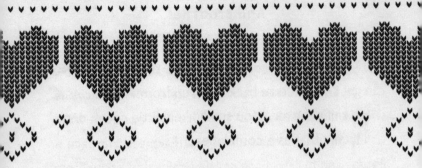

ALL HELL

'Toppest news of all time, hot off the press,' Dixie declares, as she catches up with Uggs and me in the schoolyard.

We wait for her to continue, in a prime example of how she can keep eejits in suspense.

Uggs cracks first. 'WELL?'

'Dermot and Sam Slinky are no longer an item.'

'SHAAAP!' I say. 'I don't believe it.'

'Oh, believe. It's on the grapevine *plus* I have just caught sight of her and she looks DREADFUL.'

On all levels this is interesting and a little bit delicious.

'Let's go see.'*

---

* Don't judge me, I can't help myself. And, besides, it's family business, so I have to pay attention . . .

All Hell

Sam looks v bedraggled. She is flanked by her fellow Slinkies, Dan and EmmyLou, who are warding off anyone who would dare approach. Sam's hair has gone from blonde and braided[†] to mousey and a mess. Her face is blotchy and her eyes are red, like mine, but probs from crying (in her case) and not a manky disease (in mine). The goddess don't look good!

'I did hear Dermot arguing with her on the phone,' I tell the Gang.

'Word is that she can't handle all the attention he's getting from women because of his new showbiz lifestyle. So she gave him an ultimatum and, instead of commit, they split.'

'How do you find this shizz out?' Uggs asks.

Dixie shrugs. 'It's one of my many talents. Plus, I have contacts *everywhere*.'

'Young women are flinging themselves at him, and it's only going to get worse if they make it through the semi-final and on to the final,' I confirm. 'All the lads are feeling the lurve from their fans.'

Dixie shoots me a look. 'To varying degrees,' I emphasize, remembering her (maybe) plans for the Dork.

† The Katniss Everdeen look.

'Nice to see that she's human after all,' Dixie says. 'I feel a bit sorry for her, actually. I know what she's going through.' She gives what has now become her trademark put-upon sigh, the sigh of the thwarted-in-love.

'So, what's the latest on your own, erm, love life?' Uggs asks, grabbing the perfect opportunity to check on the horror.

'Kev wants to meet up . . . and . . .'

I'm almost afraid of what else lies in store for us, but I have to find out. 'And?'

'And I kind of have a blind date that we need to go on, with the lonely-hearts Barnacle Café guy.'

There's that 'we' again . . .

UGGS: 'Which one is first?'

DIX: 'The local Lonely Heart.'

ME: 'When?'

DIX: 'Tomorrow, around five or so.'

UGGS: 'Around?'

DIX: 'OK, OK, you pair of pedants.‡ Sheesh, you're

---

‡ Didn't think Dixie knew this word or would ever use it, so I am v impressed at her show of vocabulary, despite its enclosed criticism of our attention to detail and precision.

like a tag team of annoyers. It's at 5 p.m. exactly. Choose your glad rags – we can't go in uniform.'

You know BAD and WORSE? Well, we're back there.

I lag behind with Uggs and say, 'I'm seriously thinking of hunting out Jason Fielding and fixing him and Dixie up again.'

'He'll be playing rugby with me later today, if you want to drag Dixie along and talk him up while you're watching, or whatever.'

'Or whatever': this is our plan. Slim, I know, but it's what we have to work with: rugby, it is. I shiver already at how cold it's going to be out there on the sidelines. Just as well I'm running a slight temperature still; it'll help keep me warm against the elements.

To say that Dixie is unimpressed with the prospect of standing in the mud and cold to watch boys running around after a madly shaped ball is to understate a v big understatement.

'It's for Uggs,' I say. 'We have to support him. He gets a lot of slagging off for having two female best friends, and the knitting we make him do, and all the craft-based schemes we involve him in. So we owe him. It's payback time.'

I don't know if it's my stern tone or my brilliant argument that sways her. Or neither.

'I can call it a random act of kindness,' she says. 'They're good karma.'

Whatever her reasons, Dixie comes along to the match with me.

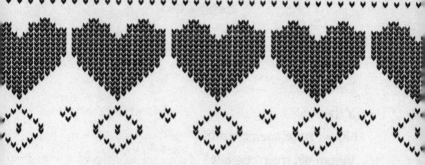

RUN RAGGED

There's quite a crowd gathered to watch the match, which surprises me. Maybe everyone is using it as an opp to be seen and check out what little talent there is in Oakdale High. I can't say I know what the rules are, but there is a lot of tussling over the ball and scrums and shouting and running at one another. The menfolk of the school are v v vocal, particularly against the referee if they feel he's got something v wrong, which he seems to a lot.

'Jason Fielding looks fit out there,' I try, hoping it'll reignite something in Dixie that isn't scorn.

'Hmm,' is all that gets.

'And Uggs is fast, just like he said.'

'Hmm.'

'Dork alert.'

'Where?'

Now I have her attention.

'Incoming, from the left.'

'Hello, ladies.'

'Hi, Gary.' Dixie gives a high-wattage beam. 'How are preparations for Saturday's show going?'

'Good, thanks. A long process. It's hard trying to decide on a number and then making sure it's not too difficult for all ten of us to play.'

'Fast or slow this week?' I ask.

'Dunno. There's a difference of opinion about whether we should show diversity or stick with another rockin' track.'

'Well, I, for one, am really enjoying it. Well done.' Dixie is full-on-charm gushing now.

'Thanks.' He's not paying her half enough attention and I'm worried she's going to latch on to this mad idea everyone has that it's me he's interested in. 'What's the score?' he wants to know . . . from me . . .

'Er, don't know. We're here for Uggs,' I explain.

'Do you play yourself, Gaz?'* Dixie enquires.

'Can't afford to at the moment,' he says. 'In case I injure the hands.'

'Or the face!' exclaims Dixie.

'Truth,' he says, nodding, pleased with a compliment.

Then he's doing funny handshakes with some mates. He doesn't seem worried those might injure his ability to play guitar.

'Look,' I say, pointing and trying to wrestle Dixie's attention back. 'I think Jason just scored.'

'Oh, how *very*,' she says disdainfully. She picked that up from some film and uses it whenever it's a *WHATEVER* situation. I fear Jason Fielding may be a lost cause.

There's a v rowdy element amongst the spectators. Firstly there's low-level jostling, then someone starts throwing balloons full of water around. Then Hugo Pheifer proves why he is the unluckiest boy in Oakdale: he gets hit and drenched by a missile, and it's clear that it's a special one.

'I don't think *that* water bomb was full of water,' Dixie says.

'Who threw it?'

* Yup, she has gone the Gaz route.

211

'Mike Hussy.'[†]

UH-OH.

'Not likely to be H_2O, then,' I confirm.

'No. Not at all likely.'

'At least it wasn't anything more solid than, well . . . that.'

Small comfort to Hugo, who is now soaked with Mike Hussy's pee. That poor guy is doomed to misfortune. It also illustrates why anyone watching a match is pleased when Mike Hussy is playing and not in the crowd. At least if he's on the pitch, he is only a danger to the opposing team, not free range and a pest to all supporters when he's not chosen to play.

On the way home Dixie discusses her plans for a mini makeover. 'I've seen this great article about how to cut your own hair and I thought I might try it.'

I'm hoping this is a plan for some time in the distant future, but no, oh no.

'Want to come home with me now and we can try it?'

---

† Minor bully and major pain-in-the-butt from our class who likes to call me 'Ginger', which I ignore and pray will not be adopted more widely.

'Are you sure you want to cut your own hair, Dixie? Is that not best left to a professional? You'll go mental if it goes wrong.' I don't add that I so don't want to be there for the event, and blamed for supervising a disazz (opposite of pzazz!).

She ignores my protest and, much quicker than I can say, 'I'm off,' we are in her room and I'm looking at the magazine with this most foolhardy of beauty plans. Whoever wrote this is a v irresponsible style guru. Basically, the process involves tying your hair in a ponytail high and tight just over your forehead and then cutting straight across the hair hanging out at whatever length you judge to be good. I feel vomitous as Dix takes the scissors to her locks, and even worse as she takes the elastic band off.‡

BUT . . .

Wonder of wonders . . .

It's OK! *Somehow* the shape is fine and Dixie's barnet simply looks freshly tidied up.

'If I say so myself, that is a total triumph,' she says. 'Another string to my bow.'

‡ It feels like I am watching it in slo-mo, so the agony is prolonged.

213

Just as well there are many strings to Dixie's bow, because if there was only one and it snapped, all she'd have left is a stick, and she would Not. Like. That.

At. All.

Suddenly I am all wrung out.[6] Well, it's no surprise. There's the stress of the *TFX* semi-final coming up; the worry of Dad's job and whether our SASS make-up range will do the trick; Mum's mind;[§] and Dixie's bonkers plans for l'amour. And that's just for starters. I'm only human. I feel overwhelmed. How many threads in this rich tapestry of life are in danger of becoming completely unravelled without some serious Jenny Q attention?

6 Again!
§ That seems to have gone astray.

THE HANDY HIDING PLACE

Home, even Quinn HQ, is usually a handy hiding place.
There is *usually* SOME sanctuary to be had in my room,
if I make sure to announce that I want to be left alone.*
Today, though, has other plans for JQ at HQ.

I run straight into Dermot, literally.

'Watch it, squirt,' he says, and not in a nice way.

'Gee, sorry for breathing,' I retort. And, of course, I
can't leave it at that. 'Heard the news about you and
Sam, by the way. Bummer.'

'I suppose everyone knows,' he says crossly. 'All of

* Well, that's after the teasing of everyone going, 'oooh,'
in a 'get her' kind of way.

them noseying around for info. Why can't people just stay out of other people's business?'

I don't *think* he's expecting an answer to that, so I don't give one. Probably the safest thing to do, as he's looking V cross now.

'Gary says the Guitars are having probs choosing a number.'

Wrong way to go, Jen, but it's out of my mouth before I can stop myself.

'Oh, for GODSAKE!' he roars, and thunders up the stairs and BANGS his door shut.

Normally I'd be secretly delighted to have driven my bro into a rage, but today it's oddly UNsatisfactory. I wonder if that's maturity creeping up on me, or just that I am exhausted.

'Hi, Mum, I'm home,' I call as I enter the kitchen.

No reply. She's there, right in front of me, but not a peep out of her.

'Oh, Jen, my lovely daughter, how good it is to see you,' *I* also say, loudly into the air. 'Aw, thanks, Mum, it's so good to know that you care.'

Still no acknowledgement.

The Handy Hiding Place

'MUM,' I roar, before I can stop myself.[†] 'Would you please pull yourself together and rejoin the human race!'

She looks at me then.

'I want my mother back,' I tell her. 'Any chance of that in this lifetime?'

Then Mum bursts into tears and runs, sobbing, from the kitchen.

Gran has witnessed the whole thing. 'Well, I hope you're pleased with yourself now, Jennifer Quinn, you spoiled brat.'

What? Me? Spoiled? A brat? WHATDIDIDO?

'Can you not see how depressed your mother is? Do you only ever think of yourself? You're supposed to be a young adult now. It's time for you to start taking some responsibility for the people around you and how they might feel. It's not all about you, you know.'

Shereek! Gran never speaks like this. She's supposed to be the kinda mad, old, doteypie bat we keep in the converted garage, not a speaker of truths.[‡]

† I know I should stop myself, but I suppose things have just boiled up inside me.
‡ Particularly awkward ones, the ones that are v close to the bone, the home truths.

'Get real, Jennifer. You think you're the only one who ever felt like this, the only one ever to feel abandoned or ignored or neglected? Or so misunderstood by the world? How do you think the rest of us have ever felt? How do you think we got by? You're not the first, you won't be the last. We've all experienced it. We've all been there. Now stop being a mollycoddled brat and try to appreciate that you have a great life and a great family, and right now you need to help someone who loves you very much but who's in a dark place.'

It's practically unbearable. I am lower than the lowest creature that is lowly crawling across the depth of the deepest ocean that has not yet even been discovered because it is too, too deep. I am worthless crud.

I realize I do take Mum for granted. I guess we all take our family as read = present/correct/OK, so. Don't we? It hadn't occurred to me before that this is a two-way street. When I consider this, though, I can't exactly see what reward there is in having me around, barring the odd sing-song (and Mum hasn't participated in one of those for ages), and sometimes I make her laugh (not for ages now). Other than that, it's all *her* giving *me* things, like advice and comfort and hair products and

The Handy Hiding Place

Kit Kats and, well, safety. Mum makes me feel safe. Dad does too. Our whole life in our little Oakdale house is where I am safe, and myself, and now everything is under threat, what with Mum being a stranger and Dad about to lose his job. It's scary. And v uncomfortable to realize and admit.

'Sorry, Gran. I didn't know Mum was actually depressed.' How could I have missed it, though? I must have been too wrapped up in myself. I realize I have been putting off my worries about Mum, hoping things will just get better on their own. I am so ashamed of myself. I feel tears well up. Then I see Gran is going to cry too.

'I'm so worried about her,' I blub. 'About all of us. And I miss her.'

'Me too,' Gran squeezes out, then she starts mopping her eyes with a tissue.

'I've been so distracted with *Teen Factor X* and school. But there must be something we can do.'

Something *I* can do, I think. It's time for Jenny Q to kick some (serious, emotional) ass, though what or how is beyond me.

I go to my room and Google post-natal depression

219

to see what we're dealing with here. A lot, it appears. But that doesn't mean giving in or standing idly by. I am done with that now. I bring my findings back to the kitchen and Gran.

'It seems to me we need to get Mum *moving* again, and out into some fresh air.'

Gran agrees. This calls for a Jenny Q 'to-do' list.

So, exercise, fresh air, a change of scenery – check.

Get her talking, engaged with us all again – check.

Look for a mum-and-baby group in the area and maybe she could go meet them – check.

Gran adds 'regular showers and getting dressed in something other than a dressing-gown' to the list – check.

It feels good to be proactive and I say this to Gran.

'Yes,' she agrees. 'This PND is the *mother* of all depressions, but together we will beat it.'

'I see what you did there with the "*mother*" thing,' I tell her, 'and it was v v clever.'

'I have my moments,' she says.

Action is everything now and there is no time to lose, so I go to Mum's room. She's lying in bed, facing the wall = not good.

The Handy Hiding Place

'Mum, I'm so sorry about earlier. I was totally out of line. I just feel we've lost touch and I hate that.'

She sits up and gives me a big, mummy, bear hug. 'I'm sorry too, Jen. I haven't been myself lately.'

'Tell you what. Why don't we meet for a coffee when I'm finished school tomorrow? You could walk Harry down to the Barnacle Café and we can meet there and go home together afterwards.'

It is a brilliant plan because it's where Dixie is meeting her blind date, but I can have a look at him while doing something else and text her as to whether she should turn up or not. Sometimes, j'amaze myself with my (natural) brainy intelligenceness.

Mum starts spluttering some excuse based on Harry being too young to go out.

'I am not taking "no" for an answer,' I tell her. 'We have a date. That's that.'

I leave before she can squirm out of the deal.

Now it's over to Gran to get her washed and dressed and out of the house the following day. I issue that to her as her mission, should she choose to accept it, like in *Mission: Impossible*. She does. Operation Help Mum is 'go'.

Every piece of me is tired, from my (strawberry blonde) hair to my badly painted toenails. I wedge myself into an armchair and start knitting Harry's blanket and let the rest of the world go by without me for a while.

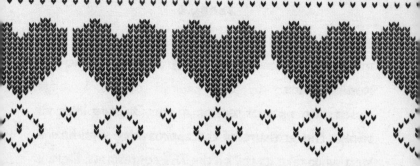

REBIRTH

Sam Slinky now has bags under her red-rimmed eyes and a crop of spots on her chin that she hasn't even bothered to pop or cover up.* She is falling apart before our very eyes. She is now a mere, teen mortal. The other Slinkies look *DAGGERS* at Dermot whenever they pass him and Sam makes as if to faint.† It's fascinating to watch. I'm not sure Dermot notices too much of it, because whenever I see him he's deep in convo with one or more of the Guitars as they try to plot their next showbiz

---

* TOTES SHOCKER!

† A kind of modern version of the 'vapours' that you see women having in costume dramas on television.

move, and so he is not really paying attention to lovelorn exes.

There is a lot of tension in the Oakdale High air today. The pressure of the approaching semi-final is starting to take its toll on the *TFX* contestants. Delia is worried about having a new routine for it. The Guitars need a song they can all agree on. The Gang is also facing problems of its own: to wit[‡] Dixie has a blind date later, which means Uggs and I do too. On the Jenny Q home front, I need to/*must* jolly my mum out of herself. My dad is nearly unemployed. And what of l'amour? Stevie Lee Bolton is even more aloof than ever because of his showbiz commitment and so even more unattainable. Gary O'Brien keeps smiling at me/ paying me attention.

To add yet another layer to things, there is another letter in the band's fan mailbox telling them they're shizz. I know it's from the same source as the first one because I recognize the paper and the writing. This one is slightly nastier, more threatening. It says, 'Be careful. When you're on that stage you are asking for trouble.

[‡] which seems to be 'i.e.' said another way – I *like* it, sounds legal and all.

224

Anything could happen.' Does that mean something is planned for the next live performance? Surely not. It unsettles me. What is this troll trying to achieve?

I have a growing feeling of apprehension as the day proceeds, and I allow my mind to wander as I sit in class. There is so much anxiety to life now. I try to visualize Harry and how happy and uncomplicated he is. I try to get some calm from that image. And when I think of him smiling, I smile too.

'Do share the joy,' Miss Harding says, when I am caught in my reverie.

I desperately try to remember what she was banging on about before I zoned out but cannot dredge anything up, so I say, 'The words, I love them. They make me happy.'

There is no way she can challenge that, even though she is a sarky weapon.

Words to the rescue, yet again. Phew for Jenny Q!

Dixie texts: **LMFO**

This is her (nicer) version of **LMAO** and is simply Laughed My Face Off and, actually, I like it better than the original rude version.

I go: **SMFO got me in trouble!**

225

I hope she figures it's Smiling My Face Off.

She returns a simple: ☺

That's her cover-all, but I think she knows what I meant.

I can taste the pasta for lunch for the first time in ages[6] and, although it's on the mushy side, it's not bad at all. We used to have tragically bad caterers,[§] but since the new lot took over there have been hardly any reports of poisoned students.

'Where are your civvies[**] for later?' Dixie wants to know.

'Ah, that,' I say. 'I have a foxy plan.'

'Do tell.'

'Well, I'm meeting my mum at the Barnacle for a coffee. She needs to get out of the house. And this way, I can enter in full disguise as a schoolgirl and check out the Lonely Heart. If he's worth it, I will say so via text, and you can change your kit and arrive in glory.'

'Good, I think. Where does Uggs fit in?'

6 Hooray, the cold is finally lifting.

§ Their fare was worthy of my gran.

** Dixie has clearly raised the Barnacle café meeting to Military Operation status.

Rebirth

'He can casually have a Coke near our mark and thusly judge him from a masculine perspective and report all to you.'

'What happens to me if he's a total loser?'

'You come in and have a coffee with Uggs, in uniform, and no one but us will be any the wiser.'

'Weirdly, Jen, I approve of your schemey scheme.'

Surely this day is going too smoothly now? Gran says you shouldn't look a gift horse in the mouth, so I won't, though it must be noted that the Trojan horse that was sent by the Greeks into the besieged city wasn't v good as a gift for the people of Troy to whom it was sent. Just saying.

As I'm leaving school I see the Guitars heading towards the Assembly hall to practise. They all carry a guitar and look grim and determined. Entertaining people is a tough business, plus they have internal frissons and disagreements that must be taking a toll.

I ring home using a code I have agreed with Gran. Two rings, then hang up, then ring again. She knows then that it's me on Mumwatch and answers.

'She's up, washed, dressed and gone out with Harry. WE are GO.'

Phase One has been a success. Now it's over to me.

Mum looks around like she's never seen the café before, even though she has. A lot has happened to her since she was here last, so maybe it looks a bit alien. I seriously doubt it has seen even a lick of paint since then and the menu certainly hasn't changed. I order a cappuccino and a slice of carrot cake from Mr Barnacle, who narrows his eyes at me. If I had been alone, or with Dix and Uggs, he'd have insisted on cash up front. He's been caught out a few times by school kids eating lots they can't afford to pay for.

'I've just had some cheesecake,' Mum says. 'At this rate I'll never lose the baby fat.'

Magazines don't help, with all of those pics of celebs looking skinny again only a few weeks after having a baby. It is added pressure on normal human beings like my poor mum. It's kind of odd that her face looks so drawn yet she has a plump body, like someone put the wrong head on her this morning.

'You look great,' I tell her.

I covertly scope the joint to see if Dixie's date is here. There is no one who looks likely.

Rebirth

'I've been meaning to ask about this,' Mum says of my bracelet.

'It's a friendship band that the Gang made in support of Ten Guitars. We used the colours of the hats I knitted for Dermot and Harry for Christmas and now we sell them at school to the Band fans.'

'We should get a tiny one for Harry. He's their Number One fan.'

'Consider it done, Mrs Quinn,' I say. 'I'll make that one myself.'

'It's so strange to be out,' she tells me. 'For a while there I thought I might never leave the house again.'

'I'm not surprised, the weather was totes shizz recently.'

'Yes, but it was more than that. I got into a rut of thinking this would be the last of this and the last of that.'

It's v strange to sit in front of your mum and have her open up like this. Don't get me wrong, I'm thrilled. It has been so long since Mum and I talked properly. And Gran and I did say we needed to get her talking again, but I am thirteen years old, not a grown-up, and I realize when we usually talk it is generally about me.

I am a little lost with this new way of things where Mum tells me how she is feeling. What do I do? What do I say to her? Nothing, I'm guessing, and I really hope that's the right thing! But it's really good that she feels comfortable enough to talk to me in such a way, though. We're pals.

'It's like everything has become the "last" time I'll do something. When Harry was born, I thought, "Well, this is the last time I'll give birth. This is my last child." And I don't want that to be a sad thing, but it's sort of taking over and heading in that direction.'

'In fairness, Mum, you thought I was your last child for thirteen years. And you were wrong.'

Mum actually laughs – a genuine, happy, delighted laugh. I am so thrilled!

'Jennifer Quinn, you are a clever little lady. That's true.'

We're both grinning widely.

'Precocious is what Gran says I am. Cheeky.'

'Just like her,' Mum says.

The idea that I might be v like my gran is not one I want leaving this table, so I am glad we are not on home territory. What's said in the Barnacle, stays in the Barnacle.

Rebirth

'Mind you, I sort of hope Harry is the last. Childbirth is scary, but most of all it hurts like hell, whatever way the baby comes out.'

'Eating, Mum,' I say, indicating my carrot cake.

Why is it that unsavoury topics involving human 'functions' often accompany meals or a snack? And while I'm at it, much as I love Harry, I'm not sure I'd be thrilled to have a new brother or sister regularly from now on. There are enough Quinns to deal with at this present moment in time.

Uggs sneaks in and sits at the back of the café and immediately holds the menu over his face. He might as well be wearing a trench coat and dark glasses and have a badge that says 'amateur sleuth' for all the subtlety he displays. Mr Barnacle is on to him in an instant. It is as if he *smells* trouble. He pockets cash for whatever Uggs has had to order to be able to stay in the establishment.[††]

A few moments later a geeky type in a parka comes in, looking around expectantly, and sits in a window seat. He places a copy of the local paper prominently on the table in front of him. The place is filling up now

[††] I hope Dixie appreciates such dedication to her cause.

231

and he looks nervous about keeping a space for his date.

He's no oil painting but he's not a mutt either. However, there is one major detail that Dixie *would* have probs with. Mainly the fact that this guy is in a class below us at school and therefore a kid! All in all, not the sophisticated gent that Dixie needs to wipe the eye of Jason Fielding! He might be v nice but the clincher is he is *twelve*, i.e. *so* not happening.

I text: **won't do, stay in uniform**

Uggs must have a similar opinion because next thing Dixie is through the door, resplendent in Oakdale maroon, saying, 'Hi.' Uggs joins us and we have Gang plus Guests. I feel sorry for the date and I can tell the others do too. He is too young to be worrying about love. All the same, we send positive vibes his way and I hope he doesn't have to wait too long for them to work.

Harry stirs while we're telling Mum about Hugo Pheifer's latest mishap with the wee-filled balloon. He's hungry. So Mum picks him up and starts to feed him – natch. I am scalded with embarrassment, of course, even though you can't really see any of her boobage because she has tucked Harry under a vast blouse she is wearing that handily unbuttons in the right area.

After a while, Mr Barnacle comes over with a *face* on him and asks if she could stop. I feel even more scaldy, though I'm furious with his attitude. Who the fajita does he think he is? We're customers and we're not bothering anyone. In fact, no one has mentioned Harry being tucked into the blouse and on to the buzoom.

Something in Mum changes, like she's getting some steel in her veins. She also has a glint in her eye that I haven't seen in a while, and this manager would do well to heed it.

'Why?'

'Sorry? Why what?'

'Why do you want me to stop?'

'We don't allow breastfeeding on the premises.'

'Why?'

'Why what?' again, from Barnacle.

'Why not?'

'It's, erm, upsetting to the other customers.'

Mum's voice gets a little louder. 'Why?'

'Em . . .'

'It's the most natural thing in the world.'

233

Well, now we have attracted the attention of the whole café. I slide as far down in my chair as I can go without sitting under the table.

'Madam, it is not allowed. It's not . . . hygienic.'

'I *beg* your pardon?'

'I mean, it's . . . not food bought on the premises, so it can't be consumed here.' This final argument from the management is as brilliant as it is preposterous.

'That's just stupid,' I hear Uggs say.

'I agree,' says Dixie.

I stand. 'Mum, let's leave.' They look at me as if I am betraying the Cause.[‡‡] I raise my chin and my voice to say, 'I don't want Harry staying here a moment longer, he might catch something nasty from this place.'

We gather our things and leave with our heads high. At the door, Mum turns and says, 'I'll be back.'

Uh-oh, that place has not seen the last of Mrs Quinn. She's in Terminator mode.

But she did say she's coming back! That means on all levels, I just know it! I text Gran **phase 2 more or less a success** and get back **HRA!** I'll explain the

---

‡‡ Not the Manager, obvs. He looks relieved that he has an ally, although I am not – I just hate confrontation.

 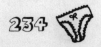

complexities of using the word 'success' when I see her, as it clearly comes laced with trouble — Mum has a hatching-a-plan look about her that doesn't bode well for all mankind, especially Mr Barnacle.

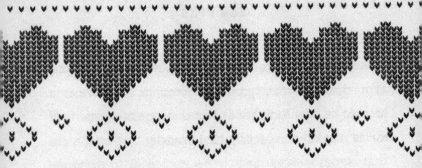

FUSSY HUSSY

In normal* circumstances, we would just pack up and go, leaving an angry whiff of sulphur behind, but this is the café visit that keeps on giving. We halt outside, as Mum is fuming and muttering to herself, Harry is complaining about his interrupted meal, and we click various bits of the baby's buggy together. Suddenly we are hit by an overpowering smell of body spray and Uggs nudges me in the ribs. When I look, who should I see wandering *ever so* casually into the Barnacle but Mike Hussy.

It takes me a moment to compute what's going on.

---

* whatever 'normal' is - I long for it and the relaxation it just *must* bring along with it.

Hussy is dressed in civvies and seems to be looking around for something . . . or *someone* . . . There isn't anyone he wants to join, so he leaves again and spots us still trying to get the enormous amount of equipment that comes with a baby in order and ready to go home.

'Hey, Ginge,' he says to me. I cringe. Although I also note that 'ginge' and 'cringe' rhyme and I might use it for one of our poetry slams some day.

'Mike,' I acknowledge.

'Is that the latest?' he says of Harry.

'Yes.'

Mum clocks Hussy and asks him his name and, wonder of all wonders, he blushes and goes all stammery.

'Nice b-b-b-baby,' he tells her.

'Thank you,' Mum says, and he goes even more crimson.

It's surreal to see him like this, like reality has been bent out of shape but is still recognizable.

I really wish he'd just bog off, though. The smell of whatever he sprayed himself with is rank: it would have been better for the world if he had just washed himself and avoided covering one pong with another.

Uggs is in with, 'Were you looking for someone in particular in there?' His face is a vision of boldness and a beamy smile is about to break out across his face.

Dixie gives him a murderous glare.

'Nah,' goes Hussy. 'Just passing, so I thought I'd take a look in.'

None of us Gang can meet the others' eyes. This must be Dixie's Lonely Heart. HAS to be! I feel like I might burst from trying not to laugh.

Mum goes, 'Got it,' as the last of the bits of the buggy click into place and we make for home, with Dixie leading a quick march.

'Mike Hussy must be . . .'

'NO!' She even holds up her hand to halt that line of talk. 'Nonononono. NOnononono. Do *not* go there. Besides, it couldn't be him. For one thing, he was way late for a five o'clock rendezvous, so it is so not him. Couldn't be. NO.'

'Could *so* be,' Uggs says.

'Au contraire, Eugene,' she tells him.

'Oh, contrary, more like,' Uggs mutters and I get a fit of the giggles.

Who would have thought that Mike Hussy, of all

people, was on the search for love? Wonders truly will never cease, though I think Dixie will cease placing adverts in the local schools' rag now. So, while one thing is a relief, the other is worrying, i.e. Hussy on the hunt for a 'significant other', a fact that means he actually does have a heart after all.

By the time we part company at our gate my ribs ache from holding in the laughter. Dixie is livid with how her brilliant plan has gone so totally awry and Uggs risks death with the cheeky grin plastered across his mush.

'Laters,' she tells us as she disappears down the street and it sounds distinctly like a threat.

Gran wants to hear all of the Barnacle adventure.

'I'll tell you something for nothing,' Mum begins, and that never bodes well. If Mum wants to tell you 'something for nothing', someone is in big doodah. It also means she is planning retribution.

'Watch this space,' she warns when she's done telling Gran of the villainy and injustice we have encountered.

'Good outcome,' Gran whispers to me. 'She's furious. That should take the shine off the depression for a while.'

I look over at Mum. Harry is attached to her boobage and she is tapping two fingers on the table as she formulates her next move. Gran's right: there is fire in Mum's eyes again!

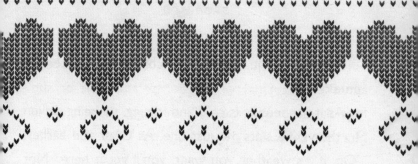

SECONDS OUT

The tension is high on the day of the second *TFX* heat. Tonight is the semi-final, two acts will go home, and next up is the final, when three more will be eliminated during the show and a winner announced. In many ways, it is a short and brutal process, and that's probably another reason the show is so popular.

It is Show Saturday and Dad drives me to the venue at lunchtime. I could easily get the bus but Dad wants to run through how we might test out the SASS range again, even as an idea.

'I am going to ask Mel if I can hand out these surveys to the kids waiting in the queue. The surveys ask kids to rate the SASS products between one and five. Then they can hand the sheets back in before they enter the studio.'

As it happens, it is cold and raining, so being driven to the venue suits me just fine. As Gran said earlier, 'Oh, if it's weather you want, you'll get it here.' Not exactly sure what it was she was trying to prove, but it sounded like a wisdom and that's all she wants most of the time: to *sound* wise even if she's spouting nonsense.

I also know I don't need to be at the venue all day this time. I have a hook on how it works and I can deal with my end of things in less time this week. Also, far more pertinently, I hate having to get up so early on a Saturday – that's just wrong. A lie-in is a lie-in is a lie-in and to be savoured fully.

I feel like wearing a mask or a scarf over my nose and mouth today to protect against any further germs lurking to pounce on me, but it's not a good look for any top Showbiz Secretary. I must take my chances. Mel is v glad to see me. I quickly fill her in on our SASS survey idea.

'Ooh, you are resourceful, aren't you? Leave it with me. So long as the surveys are distributed outside the studio, it shouldn't be a problem. In the meantime you can do me a favour and help with the atmosphere in there,' she says, pointing to the Ten Guitars' dressing room. 'TENSE hardly covers it.'

'Are they still eating, at least?'

'Oh yes, no prob there, they've gone through the rations of a small army already.'

'They'll make it, so,' I assure her.

'There must be something in the air today,' she continues. 'Grumpy, grumpy, grumpy. Margo is giving everyone such a hard time, particularly the sound department. It's unreal in there. You have been warned.'

Mel has gone all Goth this week and she looks great, like something from *The Corpse Bride*, but v much alive. She's wearing so much jewellery that she jingles as she walks. Her hair is backcombed and spiked up. She smells like roses, but darkly exotic ones, with thorns and some danger attached.

I've gone for a pair of dark trousers and a jacket that nearly matches, so it looks like I'm wearing a suit, plus shirt and tie – an 'androgynous' look, according to Dixie.

'Do you mean I actually look like a boy?' I ask.

'Not with that hairdo,' she tells me.

She has put my hair in two high bunches, which she says underscore the look while complementing and contrasting with it too.*

The lads do look pleased at my arrival, especially Gary O'Brien. They have set up my little table for me and Stevie Lee brings me a Coke. I nearly faint at the chivalry, and how v v GORGE he is. Be still my (frantically) beating heart! There isn't anything left to eat, though I don't think I could swallow anything while I am busy blushing and gulping in air at the fact that SLB paid me attention. Is this ever going to get any easier to handle, I wonder.

The Guitars are gearing up for the dress rehearsal and run through the song once again. They've chosen another crackin' rock song and it's angry and loud and exciting. In fact, I'd bet they're getting rid of a whole bag of negative energy as they thunder their way through it.

I wade through the postal offers of marriage, companionship, kisses, and even have to deal with some

---

* Yes, I had to let her loose on me earlier, no avoiding it. Besides, if she's 'styling' me, it means she has less time to come up with more bonkers ideas to seek out her next crush.

 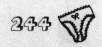

gifts that have been sent. These range from a key ring to half a bra – HALF a bra? What's the idea there? Are the two halves to be reunited as proof of who is who on a first date? Bonkers.

As I suspected, there's some hate mail (natch). I'm actually beginning to get used to this now. But that's probably not a good thing either. I don't want to excuse it. When we grow accustomed to bad behaviour, do we let it go without comment when we really should do something about it? It's probably not a good thing to ignore a problem and hope it goes away, though I prefer to do that sometimes than to act, espesh if it's an awkward situation.[†] I sigh. This makes me think of the Dixie/Kev matter. I'll have to talk to Uggs about sorting out a plan of action.

As for ignoring the hate mail, I remind myself of the threat made in the school fan mailbox. It seemed to suggest that the writer might be planning something during the show. I really don't know what to do. If I report it, I might seem like a hysterical youngster. If I don't, I'm taking the chance on the threatener being all

---

† I know I hoped Mum's problems would just get better on their own but look where that got us = lesson learnt.

mouth and no action, which I suspect they are. I think the hate-letter writer is probably more mean than deranged. I hope I'm right.

The guys are wearing black T-shirts for the performance this week and it really makes the friendship bracelets stand out. Thrillmost for me is that Dermot is wearing the beanie I knitted him for Christmas. I know I've slagged off the Dork for hat-wearing, but I am so chuffed that my bro will wear a Jen Q creation. And I know that Harry will be wearing his matching weenie beanie at home while the show is on TV.

Jess comes a-visitin'.

'How's she cutting?' she asks in her sing-song lilt.

'The lads are v uptight,' I say. 'Lot of nerves knocking about. You?'

'Grand. I'm lucky, really, because I've been writing songs since I was five and I have loads of 'em, so I'm not stuck for choice.'

'What was your first song about? The one you wrote when you were five?'

'Going to school. It's a ballad. Very sad – I didn't want to leave home.'

'What are you doing tonight?'

'A song about biros. How you need loads to suit each letter that you need to write. It's kind of a love song, y'know?'

I do, I SO do! Pens, biros, words on paper – it's my world, in a song. This Jess is a genius.

Delia arrives and greets the lads. 'I'm starving. I've eaten all my nails so I've come scavenging.'

She's out of luck, there isn't even a stray hard pear left on the catering table. She leaves in search of Mel to see if there's another delivery coming soon.

Then the day does its speeding-up thing and suddenly it's show time again. Me and the guys and Jess and Delia all do good-luck hugs backstage, then I go to my place in the audience, still shaking that I got a bear hug from SLB. Tonight Uggs and Dixie are here too, and it's funny to see how agog they are at the whole show set-up. We have about ten minutes to go when, from behind the scenes, we hear Margo saying, 'Aren't they dreadful? Bunch of spotty, hyped-up, hormonal teens.'

There is a stunned silence in the auditorium. I feel a giggle coming on. I wonder if the sound department left her microphone on in revenge for her bad behaviour

earlier in the day. There is a bit of kerfuffle as the crew and presenter realize what a terrible 'mistake' has been made, then Margo's voice says, 'Hi, everyone – just getting your attention there.' She gives a forced laugh. 'We all love one another on *Teen Factor X* but we love to do a bit of teasing too. But we're only joking. How could we not love our talented teens? It's great to see you all here tonight. Enjoy the show!'

I bet she is twice the demon now that she was before, but she'll have to play nice with everyone or be unmasked.

There is no lack of enthusiasm in the audience, even if some of the stars backstage are a bit jaded and fractious.[‡] And you'd never notice from the performances that anyone is at all below par in any area of life, especially the onstage one.

The show starts with an Oakdale double whammy – first up Ten Guitars, then Delia. We scream and cheer and wave our hands in the air for them. I have an extra layer of anxiety as the Guitars take to the stage because I know someone has made a vile threat against the

‡ Isn't that word marvellous? Got it this week from Dad, when he was talking about Dermot being in a foul humour.

guys, but the performance is so great I am transported and I forget all about the troll.

Ten Guitars do a stonking version of 'American Idiot' by Green Day but they have changed it to being Irish, so they're all an Irish-born idiot, and America is replaced with 'republic', as in Republic of Ireland. It works really well and everyone is totally rocking out the number in the audience.

The judges say it has the WOW factor and that it's totally teen and rebellious and amazing. It is, it was — the Guitars are fantasticular! It is hooray all round. But will it be enough to keep them in the show?

This week Delia talks about water and how sneaky it is. For example, how did it creep up and make us so dependent on it? It has nothing, no taste, no vitamins, no aspirin, so what's the big deal about it? And how does it get everywhere if you spill it? I can't believe how inventive and twisty her brain is. And how much I agree with her about water and how devious it is! I'm beginning to look at the world in a new way.

Jess wows yet again. She, too, has a twisty look at life. I feel so ordinary compared to everyone up there, except maybe the magician, who so has to be going home this week. He's OK, just not top-flight entertainment like the others, not inspired like them. That's me too, but I don't mind because I like the safety of my limitations – they mean I can hide and be a kid when I want to and let someone else look after me.

This reminds me that I have to look after people too. Gran said so. I've done my duty by Ten Guitars and Dad today, but Dixie also needs help, and I plan to give her some. Probably without her knowing, though – there'll be less confrontation that way. I'm all for avoiding conflict, espesh with Dix, for she is a *fearsome* opponent.

The show is brillo and the tension during the results is at a new horrific high. Margo really milks reading out the results and I wonder if it's also a tiny bit of revenge on everyone because they heard her make her boo-boo earlier. Two acts are getting the axe tonight and really anyone could go, whether they deserve it or not on their performance.

'I am in BITS,' Dixie yells in my ear.

'Me too,' I shout back.

The noise from the audience is unbelievable as they call out the names of their favourites.

Uggs is shouting 'Guitars!' and 'Delia!' in support of our Oakdale stars.

Finally it is decision time. We all hold our breath. Margo makes us wait so long we almost expire. Then *finally* she tells the magician and the dance troupe they are going home. We exhale. We scream. We will be back for the final!

Everyone, bar none, is wrung out. We have been delighted and mangled by the show. I lead the Gang backstage and we're sort of staggering from exhaustion and euphoria. It's such a thrill to flash my pass and have Uggs's and Dixie's names checked on the list to go behind the scenes – all organized by moi.

Delia looks disappointed to be through to next week.

'I've realized I may not be cut out for this,' she tells us. 'I want to be a lazyass teen, not a hard-working comic, not like this, not *national*. At least if I was doing ordinary gigs, I might have a different audience every night. With this I have to have new stuff every show – it's killing me. And I'm not enjoying it.'

Oh. My. Actual. No.

Then Gary O'Brien strolls up and gives me a

post-show hug in a PDA. Quelle horreur! I see that Stevie Lee has clocked it and he looks like he approves. I'd have hoped for just a *smidge* of envy to keep my slim-line romantic hopes alive, but no. This is all way too serious, as in:

a) that reaction and
b) the fact that this public display of affection is all the more unwanted cos it is happening in front of my Bestie, Dix, who has designs on the Dork = ARGH!

Even Uggs gives a snort of disapproval.

Like a saviour, Mel arrives with a whole box of our SASS surveys completed = phew! At least that went according to plan.

SORT IT OUT!

The new week brings good and bad all at once. Dad gets the teen make-up gig as a one-off project, but the new agency love SASS so much that they also give him two days a week work on top of that. This is v brill for me because I have:

a) helped my dad get a job and

b) I have sort of been offered a job myself too, but I don't actually have to do the work*

---

* Not yet, anyhow - in the fullness of time I'll be roped in if the past is anything to go by, and history does seem to repeat itself ... a lot.

= v satisfactory all round.

I have a stroke of luck when I get to school on Monday morning. I'm a bit early for Assembly, so I decide to put some stuff in my locker. Just as I am climbing the stairs I see a lad from the year above me putting a letter in the Ten Guitars fan mailbox and I decide to get it out as I'm passing. It is the only letter in there so far because we're after the weekend and I was my super-efficient self last week and got to the bottom of the correspondence pile. It is a letter from the troll! And I now know who that troll is.

I think I might know his reasons too. This guy plays guitar and must have tried out for the band. They only took ten – well, Eleven Guitars just doesn't have the same ring to it, does it? – so this lad didn't make the cut and he's obvs not dealing well with the rejection. I do have to act on it now, though, because this latest letter has a much more threatening tone than the rest.

I ponder my Plan of Action throughout the morning, thereby missing some French and Irish verbs and a chunk of the reproductive cycle of the frog. I know where to find the troll's classroom and then all I have to do is leave him a note and hopefully that will sort this out. Here's what I write:

> We at Ten Guitars know that you are the one leaving us hate mail. You have been seen and identified by a trusted source. Stop this activity immediately or we will report you to the principal and we will name and shame you throughout the school. We have all the evidence we need.

At lunch, I deliver the letter. I hope that's the end of it. If not, I really will give the letters to the principal and testify that I saw who put them in the box.

NEXT!

Gran texts: **Your mum has gone out with Harry to join the local mother-and-child group**

I reply: **TOP NEWS!**

It is.

NEXT!

Dixie . . .

This is a more complex problem. It's a matter of the heart. And Dixie is a cussed sort. I love her to bits but she can be stubborn and untalkable to. I'm not sure plain reasoning with her will do.

In the afternoon I miss a Maths equation, the geography of China and the conquest of the South Pole, wondering about the Dixie Dilemma.

We have a Knit 'n' Knatter in my room that afternoon as we serio need to get the hearts made for Valentine's Day.

'I hope our customers like a bit of dog hair in their love gifts,' I say as I try[†] to push Gypsy off the yarn.

'Kev wants to meet this weekend,' Dixie announces.

'Has he actually sent you a proper photo yet?' Uggs wants to know.

Dixie hesitates before answering = most unusual for her.

'I'll take that as a "no", shall I?'

'He's shy about how he looks,' she says.

'I'll bet.' Uggs is looking v grim. 'Is he as shy about how you look?'

'What do you mean?'

'Is he still looking for pics that only you and him will have?'

Her silence tells us that he is.

'He gave me his mobile number,' she offers.

† unsuccessfully - quelle surprise!

'Show us, then.'

She does and we make a note of it, as proof that he is out there somewhere.

'I don't like the feel of this, Dixie,' I say, as gently as I can. 'It's hinky. Something's not quite right.'

We knit on in silence. Then she says, 'The way things are going round here, we might not sell any of these. I'm not feeling a great Valentine spirit welling up within Oakdale.'

We knit on none the less.

We don't return to the subject of next weekend as it will only lead to a row within the Gang. It will have to be dealt with some other way.

When the others are gone, it comes to me what it is that I can do. I realize this is pretty much the same problem as the school troll, but bigger, so I need to go higher with this one. I draft another letter, this time to the police.

I write it on my computer, so it is clear and legible – besides, my hand is shaking so much with nerves that my writing would be totes rubbish. I give as much detail as I have. I voice my worries. The only thing that grieves me about it is that I will have to remain anonymous. This seems cowardly to me, like the school troll who hadn't the guts to sign up to his horrid comments, but the truth is that Dixie would never speak to me again if I got her into a big exposé and one which could only lead to trouble at home. I don't want to lose her. If that's selfish of me, then so be it. I must protect her, though – I have no choice there: it's part of my responsibility as a friend. I need to remove her from danger.

I email a copy to Uggs and text to alert him to it. I want, I need, his approval and backup for my plan. After a few minutes I get: **go for it!** I print out the letter and put it in a plain brown envelope. Uggs and Gypsy collect me and we walk to the cop shop, where we post it through the main door and hope for the best. It's up to the big boys to deal with it now.

Back at home, Mum has returned from a meeting of the mother-and-child group. She's wearing a satisfied smile that has us all as worried as the sad face she used to wear until recently.

'Anything we should know about?' Gran asks.

'Oh, you'll see,' is all we get in return.

Uh-oh. There is, officially, trouble in the air.

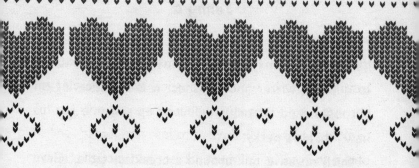

ROMANCE IS DEAD

We're doing a briskish trade in love bombs and knitted hearts in the lead-up to Valentine's Day. I'll send cards to Dixie and Uggs. I do that every year, even though I never admit to it. I'm fairly sure they know it's me, though.

The next and final (EEP!) *Teen Factor X* is the day after Valentine's and the guys want to do a love song. It will show they have range and don't just do rock.

'A very twisted love song, though,' Dermot says, 'that would be my choice.'

I wonder if that is because he and Sam Slinky are no more.

'The poet, Yeats, called love "the twisted thing", didn't

he?' This last gem is from Dad. He loves an opportunity to quote a writer and I suspect it is for showing-off purposes. And his tail is definitely up since he got his new job. He's perky.

'Such negative talk around a breakfast table,' Gran says. 'Is romance dead or something?'

'Must be,' I tell her.

Actually, Gran always gets some post on Vally's Day. She has admirers out there, even at her age!

There is a range of unexpected events on St Valentine's Day.

First up, I get a card in the post! Unsigned, of course, but I know it's not from Dixie or Uggs because I text them toot sweet and they deny it and I believe them.*

Dixie is downcast as we trudge to school. Eventually she tells us why.

'Kev has dropped off the radar. He closed his Facebook account and his phone is dead. Strange.'

'Ah, maybe it just wasn't to be, Dix,' I say, cheering inside as loudly as I ever did out loud at *Teen Factor X*. Whoever Kev is or was, and whatever he was up to, he has been stopped for now at least.

---

* can I dare to dream this might be SLB?

At school Samantha Slinky looks blonde and shiny and glorious. She is returned to her former self. Her Rottweiler-guard Slinkies are smiling. Dixie rallies from her low spirits and goes off to hunt down the gossip on the grapevine. She returns to tell us, 'Dermot and Sam are an item again.'

It's like the old order has been restored. Like the prince has kissed the sleeping beauty and the nasty spell is broken.

We have just arrived in our classroom when Jason Fielding comes through the door with a single red rose and hands it to Dixie. 'I'm sorry, babe,'[†] he says. Before I can look away they've got into major tongue snoggage that is upsetting at any hour and *particularly* pre-elevenses.

When she emerges from her clinch, all breathless, she says, 'Well, if R-Patz and Kristen can give it another try, so can we.'

All morning my mind is branded with the image of that snog = v unsettling.

I scour the canteen for Stevie Lee B at lunchtime, hoping that the sight of him will help erase the mental

---

[†] He gets away with calling her 'babe' yet again = un-be-lieev-able.

261

picture of the Dixie/Tongue snog and tell me if it was him who sent me the card. It's a long shot, I know, but, to paraphrase the saying, 'while there's lurve there's hope'!

I finally spot him. He's in a group with the Slinkies. In fact, he is *with* a Slinky. They are laughing and smiling. He puts his arm around Danielle's shoulder and I see that she is holding one of our love hearts. My world crashes into smithereens.

'I think I'm going to be sick,' I whisper to Dixie.

'I'm so sorry, Jen. I couldn't tell you he'd bought one in case it wasn't for you. I couldn't break your heart like that.'

No need, I want to tell her, he has already broken it. It feels like it has been torn in two. In reality, I have been waiting for this day for ever. I knew it would come. It had to. And the only betrayal of me is by me. Stevie Lee Bolton never promised me anything. He has never been anything but nice to me, sure, but he hasn't led me on either. I must settle for knowing that he likes me, thinks I'm a quirky little nut job, the shrimpy sister of his best friend. And if that's all it is, then that is all I get and I have to accept it. It will take time for my poor heart to heal but maybe that can happen. Maybe some day I'll get over him.

The happy group is laughing and canoodling when suddenly SLB catches my eye and holds me in his gorgeous gaze. It's like I'm mesmerized and cannot look away. Then he gives his group a glance and looks back at me, giving a little raise of his eyebrows, as if to say, 'What the hell.' It's confusing, very confusing, but I feel connected to him just enough for this agony to be a little more bearable. Then I remind myself that perhaps there is a tiny part of me that is relieved. Would I really be ready for a real-life relationship? It doesn't lessen the torture of seeing a Slinky draped around SLB, though.

Gary O'Brien appears, shuffling nervously, which is odd for him. He normally attacks any situation with confidence.

'Happy Valentine's Day, Jen.'

'If you say so,' I manage.

'Erm, I was wondering if you were going to the poetry jam next week?'

'Yeah,' I say, although I had quite forgotten about it with everything else going on. 'Why not?' I murmur,

hardly noticing my reply.

'See you there, then.' He laughs gormlessly. 'It's a date!'

WHAT! No, that is NOT what I meant . . . Oh, well, I haven't the resolve or the sheer interest to correct him.

I drift aimlessly through lessons, learning nothing, swaddled in the numb of heartbreak. Then I am rudely jolted from my woe-filled miseries by Uggs and a copy of the local paper.

'More replies to Dixie's advert?' I guess.

'Not quite,' he says. 'This is more front-page news.'

'OK . . .' It is then that I see that he is holding the *local* local paper and not our schools' one.

'You know that mother-and-child group your mum joined?'

'Uh-huh.' Now he has my attention.

'Well, here they are . . . in the news. Making the news.'

The front-page picture is of a group of breastfeeding mothers protesting in the Barnacle Café, all with their chestage proudly on show, all with a baby latched on. Oh My Actual Mother. Well, she did tell that manager she'd be back, and she has kept her word/threat. Mum and Harry are rebels, taking a stand. I know we wanted her to engage with life again, but this isn't quite what I had in mind. I just wanted her to get washed and dressed and out of the house for a nice walk every day, not to change the blooming world. Is there no end to what the Quinns can and will get up to?

It's a lot to deal with, especially on top of a broken heart. But I am proud of Mum, none the less, even if I am not exactly thrilled to see her chestage splashed over the front pages for all to behold.

THE FINAL ACT

Life goes on: that's one of the toughest things to handle about it. Valentine's Day has passed and, even if my heart is shredded, I have a few more bob in my piggy bank from the sales of our love hearts and love bombs. Love has actually bombed for me, but I am still breathing (raggedly), still moving (clumsily), still keeping on (somehow).

Finals day for *TFX* has arrived and I have to make an extra effort to look human, nice even. Just because Stevie Lee B is not going to have a big life-changing moment and realize I am the one for him,* that's no

* Le sigh. Yes, I am having romantic delusions and fantasies about him, more than ever now = MEH!

excuse to let myself go, as Dixie is reiterating for the umpteenth time. Today's ensemble is another 'nearly' suitie, a jacket and skirt that nearly match, with a little white T-shirt and my hair a bit mad. I think my nutty barnet looks a bit like the inside of my head right now, all wonky and confused.

Dixie stands back, delighted with her work, and declares, 'Chic happens!'

I drag myself into the venue, trying to look all business-like with my folders and pens. I still have a job and today the stakes are at their highest.

'Any valentines?' Mel asks.

'Yeah,' I say. 'Just the one. Don't know who it's from, though.'

She gives me a beamer and says, 'Oh, I think it's fairly obvious.' Her eyes travel to the Dork O'Brien.

'No!'

'Yes! Bet you anything.'

I look at GOB and realize that it might have been him. It does nothing to ease my anguish. I can't just replace Stevie Lee in my affections. And Gary O'Brien is not any sort of worthy substitute.

Margo is being extra nice to everyone after her v

public faux pas last week. It's a bit freaky. It doesn't suit her, TBH. She's better at being spiky and tough than a nice person.

And if the semi-final was tense, this week is off the scale. As if to mask their anxiety, the lads eat more than ever before, though they talk a lot less. There are internal divisions that are becoming clear for all to see. Like Delia says, 'Showbiz is no biz if you're not enjoying it . . . then, it's just showshizz.'

We do our last group hug as Team TG and Stevie Lee Bolton says, 'Thanks, Jen, you've been FANomenal.' It's cheesy and if the Dork had said it I would have snorted in derision but, pathetically I know, I am grateful for any crumb of attention SLB gives me.

When I join Uggs and Dixie in the audience for the show, I feel like I am a different person from the kid who came through the doors all those weeks ago. I feel more grown up. When the show music starts, though, I get a tingly excitement and I start to shout and scream like everyone else.

Delia is up first and follows a Valentine's theme. She does a routine about how tough and perverted love is. It's like she's baring my soul, but she makes it gruesomely funny too. I am laughing outside and kind of crying inside. She is *so* clever!

Next Jess has written a number about her cat sending love messages to her, including a half-eaten lamb chop, pulling threads in her sweater and coughing up a hairball on to her lap. It's funny and catchy and it nearly makes me forget my own romantic woes.

When Ten Guitars take to the stage, I feel myself freeze. This is it. It's difficult to breathe. My heart aches. They all sit in a semicircle and start a romantic number called 'More Than Words', which a band called Extreme used to sing yonks ago. It's a v beautiful melody and has lush harmonies and lovely guitar playing.

The Guitars' song would melt a stone. The judges LOVE it. The audience LOVES it. I LOVE it, and I want to hear it again and again. I think my heart might break to see SLB singing a love song. It's the last time they'll perform on the show unless they win, and you can see the tension on their faces – and feel it all around in the studio.

The night is a whizz-by blur, but finally it is time for the results. The usual agony of the disqualifications leaves the ultimate agony – the final three are Jess, Ten

Guitars and Delia! Then the show only goes and takes an ad break. WHAT?! We all squeal and howl.

I feel like I have been stretching to beyond breaking point. Uggs puts an arm around my shoulder.

'Hang in there, Jen,' he says, and I don't know if he's talking about life and love or the fact that all my faves are in the last three.

When the show resumes, the acts are standing on the stage again, looking exhausted. Margo announces that in third place is . . .

Long pause . . .

'DELIA THOMAS!'

We go nuts for Delia. Then we see all her best bits. We go nuts again.

And in second place is . . .

An even longer wait now, because this will reveal not just second place but also the winner . . .

It's . . .

Another even *longer* pause . . .

The auditorium goes weirdly silent with only one or two voices shouting the names of the final two.

And second place goes to . . .

Longest pause *EVER* in the history of television . . .

The Final Act

'TEN GUITARS!'

We go nuts! We're jumping up and down, screaming, grabbing those next to us. Onstage, the lads hug one another and look oddly relieved. Jess is crying, even though it means she has won – hey, maybe *because* she has won. We see the best bits of Ten Guitars on the show and it is thrilling to be reminded of their journey from the pavement outside the trials[†] to the live shows. The lads all raise their guitars in the air and Dermot shouts, 'Thank you, everyone.'

Then Jess, the tiny sprite from Cork, dries her eyes and prepares to sing again. She brings the house down. Jess is a true star.

And suddenly the *Teen Factor X* adventure is over. It is a v v emotional time but at least everyone is in bits, so I don't stand out as being any worse than anyone else.

Delia simply says, 'Thank Friday night that's over.'

† The tryouts I fainted at – Dixie gives me a playful dig in the ribs and Uggs gives an extra-big squeeze.

271

REAL LIFE

The ideal of a normal state is elusive to all at Quinn HQ. How come we're incapable of doing ordinary things without the world noticing what we're up to? Mum is determined to breastfeed in public wherever it is frowned on. She's part of a small army of mums doing guerrilla raids on what they see as enemy territory. Harry is oblivious to the fact that he is a poster boy for a Breast is Best militancy. He's just happy to be fed, burped, changed and talked to. There are times when I envy him the simplicity of his life.

Although Ten Guitars have decided to take some time out from being Dublin's hottest boy band, Dermot, SLB, the Dork and a couple more lads have a new group called Faction, and that's in keeping with the rebellious nature of the Quinns right now.

Dad has decided to 'confront his image', by which he means continuing his hobby of photography, in other words taking photos of us all when we don't want him to. Gran is egging him on, of course, and has suggested they do a joint exhibition of their 'work'. He doesn't seem appalled by this idea, though I am. I will always be one to champion a creative pursuit, but I am not sure I can cope with any more pics of the Quinn family on show to the public.

Gran has also decided to grow fruit and veg in the back garden and there is even word of getting hens. We'll be the Oakdale hillbillies!

At school, the status quo returns, with all the various people who need to be together being together. The Slinkies are unbearably smug, even EmmyLou, who is as single as I am, for frippsake! It's ridic.

A worrying thing happened on the way into class yesterday. Mike Hussy came up to me, clicked his tongue suggestively and winked. EEP! That sort of romantic attention I can do without, thanks all the same. I needn't have worried that he had changed utterly, though, because he gave Uggs a black eye during the rugby game after school. It's already a stunning shiner and I suspect Uggs is at least half proud of his war wound.

'I think it might be safest to get on the same team as Hussy from now,' he told us at Knit 'n' Knatter. 'Though, apparently, that's no guarantee of immunity from attack and bodily harm.'

I was busy knitting Harry's blanket at the time and it took me a few moments to realize that Gypsy was actually lying across one of my legs. Again, a worrying development.

We're falling back into our routines at home and at school. But here again there is room, still, for a surprise or seven. Today at the poetry jam GOB takes to the floor with a rap about life and it doesn't take long for everyone to cop who he is rapping about:

> Her Mum is an ACTIVIST
> She's a LACTIVIST
> Her Dad is wordy
> And that is worthy
> She got a bro

Real Life

He called Dermo

He a gee-tar-playin' man

They got a little dude

He got da attitude

He got rebellion in his soul

She got a granny

In her famlee

There are many

There for Jenny

Jenny Q

Dis foh u

WORD UP!

I am mortified but weirdly delighted too, and find myself laughing. We give a round of applause to our school comrade and I feel grateful to him.

Maybe the Dork is not such a dork after all.

If you want to learn to knit like me,

then here's how!

I'm lucky with my knitting projects cos Dixie supervises me and shows me how to do things. It's great to have someone do that for you, but if you don't, fear not, there are also books that explain everything knit-wise, like *Purls of Wisdom* by Jenny Lord (published by Penguin Books).

It's always best to do a tension square first before you embark on a project, just to check your measurements. Some people have a looser tension than others and have to adjust a pattern accordingly. And the yarn you use will have details on the wrapper too, suggesting the size needles you should use to make a 10cm square.

None of that is TOO important for the patterns I am going to give you now, because they're not for clothes and so don't HAVE to be exact.

JEN'S BATH MAT

So, I ripped up my old duvet cover – the strips are 2cm wide and I used pairs of strips tied together to make a long yarn. I like that the knots stick out of the rug and Dixie says it's good texture (which sounds v swish to me).

I used 8mm needles – these are quite big, and though I was slow knitting with them, the fact that they're a big size meant I felt I had done loads even after only a few rows.

Cast on 26 stitches. Knit every row (this makes a nice ridged finish) for about 100 rows. Cast off and, hey presto, you have a lovely BATH MAT.

It is not a very big mat (though it is heavy when you get near the end), but it is v v lush, I think (all depending on what you have recycled to make it, I guess).

HARRY'S BLANKIE

I used a slightly chunky yarn with 6mm needles. You can have all kinds of colours going on in this piece. Basically, you want a whole load of squares, and I found that 14 stitches and 18 rows made 10cm squares.

I knitted some of them all knit rows, so they turned out ridged like the bath mat (Dixie tells me this is called garter stitch). Others I did 1 row knit, 1 row purl (which is stocking stitch), and then you can either show the back or the front of the square for that texture Dixie is so fond of. And the last combo of stitches I did was this:

With an even number of stitches,
Row 1 = knit 1, purl 1.
Row 2 = purl 1, knit 1.

This makes 'moss stitch', according to Dixie, and it looks great.

I made 20 squares. When I had finished them, I laid them out on the floor and moved them around until I was happy with how they all went with one another, and then I sewed them up. If you find you haven't got a big enough blanket, you can just add more squares till you're happy with the size. When you're sewing wool/yarn use a special, blunt wool needle so you don't split the yarn.

LOVE HEARTS

The size of these will vary depending on your needle sizes and yarns, so it's a bit of an adventure. Make 2 of the following for each heart:

Cast on 4 stitches.

Knit 1 row.

Next row, knit 1, then knit into the front AND back of the next stitch so you have made a stitch. Knit as normal until the second last stitch. Knit into the front and back of next stitch to make another stitch, knit 1 = 6 stitches.

Knit 1 row.

Knit 1, knit into front and back of next stitch, knit till second last stitch, knit into front and back of next stitch to make a new stitch, knit 1 = 8 stitches.

Continue like this until you have 20 stitches.

Knit 8 rows straight.

Then start to decrease your stitches by knitting the first two and the last two of each row together till you have 14 stitches.

Cast off.

To make up, put both 'hearts' together with stuffing in the middle (use old rags or bits of yarn), then topstitch the edges all round to seal the heart. When that is done, sew the middle of the top of the heart in a tight little loop so that it makes an indentation and therefore the shape of the top of a heart. This is also handy for slipping a ribbon through if you would like to hang your heart on something.

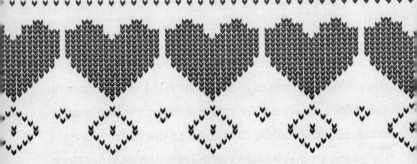

ACKNOWLEDGEMENTS

Big thanks go to all who have aided and abetted Jenny's latest adventure in life, especially those whose names I have used again and from whom I may have borrowed phrases. At Puffin, Shannon Cullen, Anthea Townsend and Wendy Shakespeare have been brill, also Daphne Tagg for her copy-editing and Sarah Chadwick-Holmes for the design. My agent Faith O'Grady and my husband Richard Cook have been endlessly supportive throughout the process, and Alice and Brenda (my cats) tried to help me by lying all over my laptop and printouts while I was writing.